Second Taste

The Book a Break Short Story Anthology 2018

Compiled and edited by Curtis Bausse

Cover design by Madeleine Prince

We write to taste life twice: in the moment and in retrospection.

Anaïs Nin

The stories in this anthology were based on the prompt to the 2018 Book a Break short story competition:

Nourishment.

Second Taste

The Book a Break Short Story Anthology 2018

Copyright © 2018 Curtis Bausse. All rights reserved.

The copyright of each story published in this anthology remains with the author.

The copyright of each illustration remains with the artist.

All rights reserved. No part of this publication may be reproduced, distributed, or transmitted in any form or by any means, including photocopying, recording, or other electronic or mechanical methods, without the prior written permission of the publisher, except in the case of brief quotations embodied in critical reviews and certain other non-commercial uses permitted by copyright law.

This is a work of fiction. Names, characters, businesses, places, events and incidents are either the products of the author's imagination or used in a fictitious manner. Any resemblance to actual persons, living or dead, or actual events is purely coincidental.

All proceeds from the sale of this book will go to the Against Malaria Foundation.

Second Taste

Table of Contents

Foreword	1
Judge's Preface	6
The Sad Tagine by Laura Theis	8
The Light of Their Lives by Boris Glikman	16
Lucky Tea Stall by Gayatri Swaminathan	23
Harvest by Arron Evans	29
The Tasting by Susanna Bellini	34
Christmas Feast by Christine Hayward	41
Branigan's Well by John Paul Davies	45
Dinnertime by Steve Wade	51
For As Long As It Burns by Tom Wolosz	57
We Are Green by Susanna Callaghan	64
It All Tastes Different Here by Emily Lomax	70
The Morbid Virus by Parker McIntosh	76
The Catharsis by Alexandra Hademenos	84
Finding the Music by Cath Barton	91
Unsent by Irma Goderdzishvili	99
Mother Nurture by Laura Geall	106
And Came the Flying Pig by Anais Jay	113
The Climber by John Paul Davies	121
Enlightenment by Kriss Nichol	128
Escaping Sephora by Moomal Ahmed	135
Done by Thomas MacColl	142
Rosie by Matt Gibson	148
Mirabelle by Susanna Callaghan	155

Learn How To Fall by Julian Cope   163
Second Chances by Parker McIntosh   169
The Tava by Radhika Borde   175
Solving Torrent's Equation by Jeremy Forge 185
The Gold Mystery by Brian Gosling   200

Foreword

What do Audrey Ellis and Alain Krivine have in common? They saved me.

Now, you may not have a clue who either of them is, so let me elucidate.

Audrey Ellis wrote *The Hamlyn All Colour Freezer Cookbook* in 1978; Alain Krivine founded the Ligue Communiste Révolutionnaire in 1974. Needless to say, they never met, and neither of them has ever known that they saved me.

Back in the 1980s, I ran a restaurant. People I've met more recently find that astounding. 'You? A restaurant? Come off it!' They see me as an arty type who likes nothing more than to write and doesn't have the sort of brain to calculate the profit margin on a *salade niçoise*. And indeed they're right. Running a restaurant was entirely unintended.

Flashback to 1975, Istanbul. Being a hippy, I was on the hippy trail to India, along with a few thousand others. Among them was Gérard: we met in what was to be our bedroom for the next two nights, the back of a Mitsubishi pickup, itself on a cargo boat about to set sail for Trabzon. We talked about May 68 and anarchism, LSD and cannabis, Kerouac and Burroughs. And when the journey was over, we stayed in touch.

A few years later, as we wondered what to do with our lives, I said, 'I've always wanted to run a café-theatre.' 'Nice idea,' said Gérard. 'Let's do it.' So we did. Well, sort of.

By the time we got round to it, I was living in Nantes, married, with a two-year-old daughter, but my eagerness was intact. The premises we found were in an old, empty building in urgent need of repair. Having no money, we did it ourselves, following the approach recommended by my wife: start by serving food on the ground floor, add the theatre above when we can manage it. As for her own contribution, well of course she'd do what she could but she certainly wouldn't be giving up her job as a teacher. We were somewhat dubious but we couldn't deny that this was firmly stamped with common sense. And so it was that at midday, 4th May 1982, I unlocked the door and turned the sign in the window from *Closed* to *Open*. The Perroquet Bleu was born.

At 12.05 the place was full. Somehow, dazed and bewildered, we managed to provide everyone with food. The same thing happened the next day, and the next. 'Can't you open at 11.30?' people asked. 'Noon's a bit late for us.'

By the end of the week, our nerves were frazzled, the fridges were bare and the kitchen was the aftermath of a tornado. 'Phew! What a week!' I collapsed onto a chair. 'Still, we've got the weekend to recover.' We hadn't even noticed the stalls going up on the square outside: the annual antiques fair was about to start. At midday people were hammering on the door, incredulous. 'What? It's closed? I don't believe it!'

My wife was all for opening. 'We've got bread and pâté, haven't we?'

I looked in the fridge. 'We can make eight sandwiches with five grams of pâté in each. And half a gherkin.'

Reluctantly, my wife agreed: the Perroquet Bleu remained shut. 'OK. But listen up, guys. Going forward, we're faced with a choice. Lunchtime or evening? You've seen what happens at lunchtime. This whole district is packed with office workers who need a place that's quick, cheap and good. And evenings? You've been up till midnight for the sake of a dozen people. So either we get organized, go flat out for lunch and make some money, or else you pursue your pipe dream of a theatre.'

Gérard went into a sulk. He complained there was no point in voting because the result was a foregone conclusion. But it wasn't, as he thought, out of marital solidarity, nor even – though it did weigh heavily – because I wanted to be there in the evening to read *The Very Hungry Caterpillar* to my daughter. It was because my wife was again speaking common sense.

It came as no surprise when a couple of weeks later, Gérard announced, 'I've thought things over. This isn't what I signed up for, you know. I'm off.' Neither of us tried to stop him.

There followed a period of adaptation, improvisation and stress. We hired our first waitress. We asked the bank for a loan to buy an industrial dishwasher: they refused (we changed banks). We opened, as requested, at 11.30 (at 11.38 it was full). And we decided that with 80% of our customers being regulars, we couldn't do without a *plat du jour*.

So at 4 p.m. every day, after getting through a mountain of washing up so high it would take a Sherpa to scale it (the washing machine on order was for some reason stuck in Italy), I set about making tomorrow's dish of the day. For 60 people. The only problem being that up until then, my culinary skills had been limited to a mushroom omelette for four. In those days, you couldn't go online to sift through a million recipes; instead, you opened a cookbook. Some people might say their lives were changed by reading *Anna Karenina* or *Catch 22* – in my case, it was the *Hamlyn All Colour Freezer Cookbook* by Audrey Ellis. Should you ever need to cook a meal for 60, I suggest you go for a perennial favourite, beef, beer (Audrey didn't specify but I recommend Guinness) and walnut casserole. My ham jambalaya, on the other hand, was a disaster...

For all that Audrey was an inspiration, she didn't actually do the cooking for me. Come September, I was a zombie, tottering about in a stupor, wondering where my life had disappeared. Then a couple of events occurred that helped me recover it.

First the dishwasher arrived. I don't know if the Pope, appreciative of my efforts to feed the multitude, interceded on my behalf, but the Italians relented and allowed it to proceed to our kitchen. Just imagine: load the tray, turn a knob and in 60 seconds it's done! The dishwasher did to my working day what the steamship did to transatlantic travel.

Then there came an even more spectacular improvement: Annie. My sister-in-law, who until then had lived in Bordeaux, was a cook, who instantly handed me back my life by taking over the duties of *plat du jour*. She had her own recipes – *boeuf bourguigon, blanquette de veau, poule au pot* – and knew very well how to make them. Occasionally, as an Ellis devotee, I persuaded her to open the *Freezer Cookbook*, but it was only with great misgiving that she ventured outside her repertoire.

And who do I have to thank for Annie's arrival? Alain Krivine. Because anyone seeking to overthrow capitalism needs a place to plot and plan with their fellow revolutionaries until late into the night, and Krivine found it in the Nausicaa, the *crêperie* Annie had opened on the Rue Ste Catherine, one of Bordeaux's busiest streets. Delighted to help the Revolution in this way, Annie happily let them occupy the place for hours, eating the occasional pancake, while other customers would venture in, assume (quite correctly) that they'd stumbled on a private political meeting, and walk out again. Six months after opening, Annie phoned us in tears. 'My place is going bankrupt!'

'Oh, not to worry,' said my wife. 'There's a job waiting for you here.'

So thanks to a recipe book, a group of revolutionaries and a dishwasher, I survived. The experience of running a restaurant left me with a deep appreciation of the ways in which food is produced, transformed, and blended into rich, subtle flavours. The same is true of writing. And if, as Anaïs Nin says, we write to taste life twice, as readers we have the chance to taste our favourite stories as often as we like.

If I've taken the liberty of indulging myself with this preface, it's partly because, for various reasons, the Book a Break competition is no more, so this is the final anthology to emerge from it. For me it's been a highly rewarding experience: I've learned a lot about editing and publishing, made the acquaintance of some excellent writers, and read a lot of great stories. I've been fortunate in having each time a judge who is helpful, conscientious and discerning, and Sherry Morris, this year's judge, whom I sincerely thank, is no exception. As a result, I'm delighted that

Second Taste provides the same fare as its predecessors: a wide variety of fine writing and a set of stories that may be thought-provoking or humorous, poignant or provocative, but always entertaining.

Cooking and eating are common to all humanity, and such a central part of our lives that it's rare to read a book without seeing someone tuck into a meal. We eat not just to stay alive but draw vitality and develop; thus, by extension, nourishment goes beyond the consumption of calories to encompass love, spirituality and fulfilment. In *Second Taste* you'll come across all forms of sustenance, from the hope embodied in Laura Theis's prize-winning *The Sad Tagine* to the childhood memories attached to Radhika Borde's *tava*. As always, it's the characters we remember: the cunning Fenella in *The Tasting*, the obnoxious Chad in *Second Chances*, the hapless Camilla in *Escaping Sephora*. A preface can't do justice to them all, and nor should it try. The stories themselves suffice, each one a snack just right in itself.

Bon appétit!

You'll be pleased to know, by the way, that we did eventually open a theatre. And I'm still in touch with Gérard today.

Curtis Bausse

curtisbaussebooks.com

Judge's Preface

We all need nourishment. It's a simple fact of life. Without some form of it, we die.

So when I learned the theme to this year's Book a Break competition was 'nourishment', I considered myself lucky indeed. I would have the opportunity to read all the stories submitted and looked forward to feasting on a steady stream of stories that would sustain me through a long Scottish winter.

Reader, I was not disappointed.

Without doubt I relished my role. I'm always hungry for a good story, and sank my teeth into these juicy, meaty tales, indulging in a great many nourishing morsels.

The dictionary defines nourishment as *the food necessary for growth, health, and good condition*. Unsurprisingly, this anthology offers up a great many tales that involve food that will delight and tickle taste buds.

The second definition states *nourishment is the action of nourishing someone or something: the nourishment of our bodies and of our minds.*

It was stories that adhered to the second definition that, for me, offered the most satisfying read.

What I found valuable in reading all these stories was the discovery that nourishment can take so many different forms. Each tale offered something worthy and touched on the nourishment theme in its own unique way. I couldn't help but be impressed with the quality and inventiveness of the stories submitted. I appreciated and marvelled at each writer's effort and approach to the theme. I think you will too.

Within these pages you'll meet characters who find nourishment not only through food, but through travel, music, and nature. You'll read many stories where nourishment (or lack of) from family and relationships is explored. In some stories it's the protagonist who provides the nourishment rather than seeks it. It was a very difficult task selecting stories for the long list. Creating the shortlist from the banquet of stories on offer was agonising. I read and pondered over each story many times, wondering which to choose from such a tantalising smorgasbord.

The results are here now. In your hands. You're reading the crème de la crème of the nourishment stories. They will make you laugh and cry and marvel at the infinite amount of ways writers' words nourish us. I hope you enjoy these stories as much as I did.

So, reader, now that I've whet your appetite. Come to the table. Get comfortable. Bring your napkin, fork and knife. Dig in and savour these tales. You'll come away sated, likely wanting to raise your glass to these writers and thank them for providing such a satisfying read. I know I did.

To the writers who submitted a story, thank you! It was a privilege and honour to read your words. I wish you the very best with your stories and writing. I salute your perseverance. Remember, words nourish us all. So keep writing!

Sherry Morris, September 2018

Website: https://uksherka.com/uksherka/writing/

Second Taste

First Prize

The Sad Tagine

by Laura Theis

I

My story starts with a memory of my mother. My mother, the alchemist. Deliberating in front of the spice rack like an artist might in front of a colour palette. Wielding a kitchen knife, a porridge spoon, a rolling pin. Kneading dough with her delicate hands. My mother with flour on her nose and grease on her apron, auburn curls coming loose from her headband. The smell of butter and cinnamon, thyme and tarragon and lemon, roast chicken and cocoa.

'Cooking', she told me once, 'is magic. Nothing more. Certainly nothing less.'

Watching her, you would have believed it. I certainly did. It really was like magic, the way she carefully, painstakingly, combined each of the ingredients into a creation that would explode in a burst of flavour in my mouth with each bite. And just like magic, it required precision and sacrifice, training, timing, theatrics, an audience, but above all, a talent. A gift.

It made her happy to see me eat. It made me happy to watch her cook. That was how our roles were allocated. She never tried to teach me, and I never thought to ask. Until it was too late.

II

After my mother's stroke, I started hating myself in supermarkets, staring guiltily at my selection of microwavable lasagne and freezer pizza sliding listlessly towards the till.

Second Taste

'People think they can buy their food pre-packed in the supermarkets, they would have it prepared by machines and robots and then they're surprised that their lives are without wonder.'

That is the kind of thing my mother would whisper to me after peering into somebody's ready meal-filled shopping cart, her round eyes full of empathy.

Now that she was gone, everything tasted of cardboard and shoe soles and loss.

Missing my mother was like a dull and constant ache that sometimes flared up into a pain so sharp I thought couldn't bear it. I felt terribly lonely. Stay-in-bed depressed. One day my friend took pity on me and staged a mini-intervention. I should go out more, and meet some nice men, was the gist of her lecture. I was touched by her concern, so I let her talk me into putting up an online dating profile. Under 'interests' I put: *I like eating really lovely food.* I couldn't think of anything else. My friend was not too happy about that.

'I think you're being a bit too honest there,' she said. 'It makes you sound fat.' I was outraged.

'It makes me sound like someone who likes food!' I protested. 'Like a sensual woman.'

Of course, I should have listened to her. These are the kind of messages I got:

'So, you like eating? Me 2. I cld eat u out.' or *'If your left leg was Christmas and your right leg was Easter would you let me come for dinner between the holidays?'*

Dozens of them, in all possible variations.

Needless to say I never felt very tempted to meet any of these men. One guy wrote a nice message, though. He said he was applying for cookery school, and he would like to cook me a meal and get feedback. I was nervous when I met him at his place. He didn't look anything like his profile picture – so much so that I suspect he must have stolen somebody else's off the internet. He was very short and squinty with a skin condition. But his food was hearty, tasty, interesting – and it gave us something to talk about. I enjoyed myself more than I thought I would; I was even mentally prepared to forgive the profile pic deception, until halfway through dessert – honey-fried banana with vanilla and green pepper custard sauce – when he suddenly said, unsmilingly:

'So if you liked that you can lick the rest of the custard off of *my* banana.'

And then he started to undo his flies. I swallowed, blinked twice, then picked up my bag, slowly walked backwards out of the flat without saying a word, and started running. He didn't follow me. But by the time I was at home, I was crying. Then, after a while, I stopped, and pulled myself together. At least he had given me a new idea: something to do with my sorry life.

III

If cooking is magic, then the LSC (Leroix School of Cookery) is pretty much the equivalent of Hogwarts – the one place where you would go to learn how to do it. They only accept eight new students each year, and most of the graduates go on to become great cooks, some of them celebrities. Who knew? Maybe somewhere inside of me, I had inherited my mother's gift. I imagined her, how proud she would have been of me if I became the next Michelin starred chef. So I set my sights on getting in.

To apply, you need to write a statement about why you would be the best possible student they could hope for. That part was easy. I thought of my mother, and wrote down the things she would have said. I heard her voice ringing out in my mind, clear as a bell – she dictated the whole letter to me.

When I got invited to the practical exam, I was delighted, but not surprised. I knew the letter had been good. The second round was the hard part: every applicant has to cook a signature dish. To make it to round three, you need to convince a panel of three examiners. So I started to practise. Like a madwoman. I practised a single dish, over and over again, three times a day:

My mother's lamb and pear tagine.

I didn't look at any recipes, all I used was the memory of my mother making it. Trying to replicate her movements, and the way the kitchen had smelled. The way she had sliced the onions in the air, peeled the pear in one single curl. I experimented with the spice mix, created my very own ras el hanout – I knew it was right when it smelled just as it had in her hands.

When the day of the exam came around, I felt as ready as I could have. I knew my mother was watching me.

IV

I will never forget the three identical facial expressions on the LSC teachers' faces as they tasted my tagine.

'This tastes like ashes!' one of them exclaimed, and all three of them spat what they had in their mouths back into a napkin.

That was it, my budding career over.

I went home weeping, feeling dead inside. I had been annihilated, and I had official proof that cooking was not for me, never would be. It would be ready meals and yearning for the rest of my long, lonely life.

Just as I was thinking this, my phone started beeping. Its usual gentle sound, like a small bird, but a sound I had grown to hate nonetheless because of all the unwanted sex messages from the dark underbelly of online dating: Even after Vanilla Custard Guy I had never cancelled my account. I had only adjusted my 'interests' from '*I like eating really lovely food.*' to '*I like eating really lovely food* but please don't send me any aggressive sex messages I find them disturbing and scary. Thanks.'

The message was indeed from the dating site. It read: '*I recognised your picture from the LCS exam. I think I know what went wrong with your tagine. I did not get in either. Can we meet? Joe*'

I read and reread the message. I could not resist. It was too intriguing.

'*When?*' I replied.

'*8 pm. 4 Sorrel Road. Be hungry. You won't regret.*'

I bet I will, I thought, and then, like an idiot who'd never had an encounter with the custard guy, I rode my bike to Sorrel Road at 8pm.

V

The boy behind the mysterious message had dark hair, earnest grey eyes and the most striking cheekbones I had ever seen.

'I don't remember you. I would have remembered you,' I stammered instead of a hello. He smiled, didn't reply, just walked along the corridor and disappeared around a corner. I made up my mind, took several deep breaths, closed the door behind me and followed him, marvelling at myself – I had only just met this boy, and still I felt nothing but instinctive trust.

His kitchen was stunning: a bright open space with large windows and a bar with two elegant bar stools. On it, he had arranged a tiny dish.

'Samphire and salsify with globelettes of candied fennel,' he explained.

Second Taste

I could not believe what I was eating. Nothing had ever tasted so exquisite.

'What is this taste?' I asked him, speaking louder than I had meant to. 'It tastes like someone kissing you!'

'I'm glad you think so,' he replied. We both blushed. 'The next course', he said quietly, 'is what I made at the try-out exam, my signature: venison with rosehip beetroot puree and charcoal oil.'

I gasped when I saw the intricate dish, at how lovingly it was arranged on the plate.

'How could they possibly have rejected you with this!' I exclaimed.

He watched me as I assembled my first forkful. It looked and smelled perfect, but as soon as I had swallowed my first mouthful I started to cough. It was bitter and dry and impossibly salty. It tasted like dust. I chewed and chewed and could not swallow it.

'What does it taste like?' he asked quietly.

'It tastes – exactly like my tagine,' I whispered. He nodded, and looked at me expectantly, like I needed to say more. 'Like loss, and endless days, and not being able to breathe,' I said. 'Like staying in bed and having nothing to live for, not really.'

He met the question in my eyes and held my gaze.

'I learned this dish from my father,' he said. 'Cancer got him last Christmas.'

I suddenly had a lump in my throat.

'Thank you. I don't think I can finish this.'

He laughed. 'Please don't. It was only to show you what I had found out.'

'Why we didn't get in?'

He nodded. Something inside me melted and I had to dig my nails into my wrists to keep from wailing. 'What's for dessert?' I asked instead.

'Chocolate soufflé,' he replied. 'But I was hoping that maybe you could make it.'

'I have never made a cake before in my life,' I laughed. 'Let alone a soufflé! I can only make my Sad Tagine.'

But he only nodded encouragingly.

'Try it. For me. Please. The ingredients are all there…'

He made a sweeping gesture. And so I tried. I went about it like a sleepwalker, in a half-trance, in this stranger's kitchen, never doubting what I had to do, how much chocolate to melt, how long to beat the eggs. Having Joe silently watch me didn't make me as nervous as I thought. It was comforting. While the soufflés were rising in the oven, I had a sudden inspiration and picked a couple of leaves from the small basil plant on the windowsill, and added them to the whipped cream. I even knew, without looking, when the time had come to take the soufflés out.

'I didn't know I could do this,' I said while I carried the plates over to the bar. I watched Joe as he dug in.

'What does it taste like?'

He looked up at me, his grey eyes dark.

'It tastes like someone holding your hand for the first time after you've walked on your own for a very long way,' he said. 'It tastes like hope.'

Laura Theis grew up in a whitewashed house in Waldperlach's Fairy Tale district, where each street bears the name of a mythical creature. Maybe that's why you can often find a sprinkling of magic in her writing... Today, she is an award-winning singer-songwriter and her short stories, radio plays, songs, and poetry have been broadcast and published in the US, Germany and the UK.

Her new work is forthcoming in *The London Reader, Strange Horizons, Dime Show Review, About Place Journal, Enchanted Conversations* and from Three Drops Press. She is the winner of the 2017 AM Heath Prize and holds a Distinction in Creative Writing from Oxford University as well as an MA in Theater Studies, German and American Literature from LMU Munich. A regular live performer, she lives in Oxford with her scruffy black dog.

Follow her on https://www.instagram.com/wodehouse_and_i

Visit her website http://lauratheis.weebly.com

Hear her sing about mermaids, myths and monsters on https://badasssnowwhite.bandcamp.com

Runner-up

The Light of Their Lives

by Boris Glikman

It was perhaps inevitable that some bright spark in the Research and Development Department of a certain, internationally famous company would, during a brainstorming session, come up with the idea of a beverage consisting solely of pure light. The essential concept behind it was simplicity itself: why, in these modern, fast-paced times, go through the lengthy and convoluted process of needing the Sun's light to be photosynthesised by plants into chemical energy, which then has to be converted into carbohydrate molecules, which we then have to consume and digest in order for us to finally incorporate the energy from the Sun into our systems? Why not bypass all the intervening stages and just capture, bottle and imbibe the sunlight energy directly?

The management loved the proposal and supported its realisation by all means possible. Thus, less than a year after the go-ahead was given, the product appeared in the shops: a soothing, delightful elixir of natural sunshine, free of any preservatives, added sugar or artificial flavours.

The drink provided an instant energy boost, sating hunger without any necessity for digestion, as well as immediately quenching thirst and making one feel warm all over. And, of course, it was suitable for all types of diets including but not limited to kosher, halal, vegetarian, vegan, raw vegan, gluten-intolerant and fruitarian. No one could take any issue with it, for it was pure light straight from the Sun. And, fortuitously, it was also very suitable for those dieting, for according to the famous $E = mc^2$ equation, even a tiny amount of mass released a tremendous amount of energy and thus one could quaff great quantities of this potation with hardly any weight gain.

Amazingly enough, apart from satisfying the most basic physical needs (food, water, warmth) in the hierarchy of needs, this beverage also enabled the consumer, and this was a completely unforeseen consequence, to become instantly spiritually enlightened once they have drunk it and thus fulfil the highest need in the hierarchy of needs – the yearning for self-actualisation. (Perhaps it should not have been so unexpected, for, by ingesting light one, *ipso facto*, became illuminated within, which is exactly what enlightenment is, and also as the very morphological structure of the word 'en*light*enment' indicated its intimate connection to light.)

This serendipitous effect was perfect for the contemporary society, for given that the online world now provided instant information, instant communication, instant entertainment and instant gratification of needs and desires, it was only natural there would also be a great demand for instant self-realisation. And with this product, one no longer had to spend countless hours meditating and repeating the mantra, or sit at the feet of a guru, or clamber up the Himalayan Mountains in search of monasteries. Instead there was the convenience of immediate spiritual awakening in a bottle, accessible to all.

The advertising campaign was built around the slogans 'Instant EnLIGHTenment™ in a Bottle!', 'Fast Food for Body and Soul!', and 'Let the Light DeLIGHT You!'. For once the reality corresponded exactly to the promotional claims, as it truly was a unique kind of an invention, the likes of which had never been seen before.

And so, as was to be expected, everyone flocked to buy the new drink, for, apart from its obvious appeal to the general public, its attraction was also irresistible to a diverse range of people with specific needs, such as the athletic types looking for an immediate energy fix, the spiritual seekers looking for the truth about themselves and the Universe, and the weight-conscious dieters, who immediately added it to their fastidious regimens. Of course children loved it too, given its novelty value and its almost-magical properties.

This unqualified success gave the company the freedom and the impetus to experiment with new varieties of the product. The flavour of the original sunlight brand was a mixture of melon and orange. Later on, many more flavours became available, as the company's researchers went about capturing and bottling light from other celestial objects, as well as from man-made sources.

It was discovered that each planet and star had its own unique taste: Moonlight was cooler on the palate than sunlight and had an indefinable element to it one couldn't quite put a finger on; Mars tasted a bit like tomato juice; Venus was quite tart and almost vinegary, and thus was best drunk in combination with light from other sources; Jupiter and Saturn, as befitting their gaseous nature, were like the finest bubbly champagne; and supernovas had a mouth-exploding, extremely hot chilli flavour that only the very brave and the foolhardy dared to sample. It was also found that the illuminations of every city had their own particular flavour, although the health-conscious preferred only drinks made from natural sources and scorned the artificial flavours of light globes, fluorescent lights and neon signs, which invariably tasted like cheap wine.

With this product on the market, many believed the world was surely heading towards a utopian existence in which humanity would finally be liberated from its burdensome, imprisoning dependence upon plants and animals for nutrition; and the common man, having become instantly enlightened, would see beyond the constricting confines of self-interest and self-preservation and realise everything is inextricably connected and we are all one.

Yet, those who were optimistic that an idealistic state of being would at last be achieved had forgotten all about a deep-rooted and paradoxical aspect of human nature, namely that anything that brought pleasure and enjoyment was open to abuse, misuse and overuse. Consequently, the very source of gratification and bliss, like for example alcohol, could and did mutate grotesquely into a dire threat to one's very existence. Thus obesity and all the maladies it caused was rife in those societies in which food was in ready supply; alcoholism was the scourge of many a land; addictions to both legal and illegal substances destroyed countless lives.

Given the way this beverage immediately satisfied, in one neat package, a person's needs on so many levels, it was inevitable some would become hooked on it. As is often the case with addicts, they found ways to bypass the option of legally purchasing a limited quantity of the product, instead consuming for free limitless amounts by staring directly at the Sun and letting the light flow both into their open mouths, as well as into their eyes. Imbibing light through the eyes was something non-addicts would never do, and that particular experience was likened to mainlining heroin, giving an even greater kick.

These addicts quickly became known as 'sunkies' (a portmanteau word blending 'sun' and 'junkie'), and this word coincidentally had the additional connotation of 'sinking' which was very apt, for no drug addict had ever sunk as low as these sunkies. Most of those hooked on narcotics could be rehabilitated and again become respected members of a community. The Sun junkies, however, voluntarily gave up their sight and their mobility, two of the most precious and vital features a human being possesses, and assumed a static, plant-like existence, remaining rooted to one spot. They cared for nothing else but to follow with their turning heads the Sun's daily progress across the sky, using their sense of warmth to locate it, their retinas having been burnt out, and to drink in the light.

'*In Sol Veritas*' – in Sun all Truths lie – was their motto and guiding principle, believing as they did that the Sun is the portal to the ultimate reality and the sole source of eternal, absolute truths. Their proselytising spiel to the non-addicts was quite persuasive, claiming that once you started staring at the Sun, you would quickly realise how petty and drab are the affairs of daily life, and how overflowing-with-meaning and magnificent are the inexhaustible revelations and infinite beauty emanating from the Sun, the place where perfection, transcendence and purity lie. The sunkies also extolled the stability and the security their lives now possessed, for the Sun's motion, perfectly predictable for millennia to come, scorched away the uncertainties of their previous everyday existence.

One saw these sunkies everywhere one went, sitting, standing or lying on the pavements, roads, grass, in the mud, in puddles, in gutters, totally oblivious to their surroundings. Their limbs became atrophied from complete lack of movement and turned into something resembling gruesome, withered tree branches, further accentuating their plant-like appearance. The sight of these addicts was both sickening and unspeakably sad, especially as many of them were young people who had sacrificed all the promises the future held out for them.

The greatest tragedy was that the sunkies denied their lives had turned into a tragedy at all. Not only did they become physically blind, they also became blind to the reality of their situation, convincing themselves into believing they were superior beings living superior lives, the only ones in possession of the ultimate secrets of existence. They saw themselves as part of an elite caste, the vanguard of an egalitarian utopia to come, for before the Sun everyone was equal. These Sun's Sons (as they preferred to call themselves) were totally untroubled by their loss of sight and mobility, for there was nothing down on Earth they wanted or needed to see or do. Indeed they considered their blindness and immobility to be a godsend, for not only did it stop them from being distracted from giving all of their attentions to the Sun, but, even more importantly, it prevented their minds and souls from being contaminated by the imperfections and iniquities that so marked and defined earthly existence.

Thus, light in a bottle, previously the greatest blessing to mankind, became its greatest curse, causing a calamity the likes of which could not be imagined before its arrival on the market, for who could ever envision healthy people willingly becoming immobile vegetables, sacrificing their lives just so they could stare at the Sun and feel its warm smile upon their faces? In the bitterest of ironies that occur so often throughout the course of history, mankind, having liberated itself from its dependence upon plants, and thus attaining the greatest freedom it had ever possessed, now found an ever-growing proportion of its population choosing to lead a plant-like existence.

But this unfolding global tragedy was of little concern to the company that brought the beverage into the world, for its technicians were busily working on an even greater creation which would undoubtedly trump the bottled sunshine for popularity. Inspired by instant coffee and instant noodles, the new invention-in-the-making already had the brand name of Insta-Life, and, once completed, it would allow a person to experience their whole life in an instant. This surely was, or so the management reasoned, the ultimate desire and goal in this instantaneousness-obsessed era, for by condensing all of your life into one single moment, you would no longer have to trudge through decades of endless drudgeries and tediously repetitive routines of daily existence, through all the banal and boring stretches of life, and instead get it over and done with in a jiffy. Additionally you would gain an unbeatable upper hand over your rivals in the field of fast living.

With the lure of holiday profits in their minds, the management kept prodding its engineers and scientists to work harder and harder, so that Insta-Life could appear on the market around Christmas time. And so it was only a matter of time before this new invention swept the world, and people would begin to live and die faster than mayflies.

Boris Glikman is a writer, poet and philosopher from Melbourne, Australia. The biggest influences on his writing are dreams, Kafka and Borges. His stories, poems and non-fiction articles have been published in various online and print publications, as well as being featured on national radio and other radio programs.

Boris says: "Writing for me is a spiritual activity of the highest degree. Writing gives me the conduit to a world that is unreachable by any other means, a world that is populated by Eternal Truths, Ineffable Questions and Infinite Beauty. It is my hope that these stories of mine will allow the reader to also catch a glimpse of this universe."

Blog: https://bozlich.wordpress.com/

Second Taste

Runner-up

Lucky Tea Stall

by Gayatri Swaminathan

He hurried up to the counter – she stood there, his first customer as always – her eyes were more tired, her skin greyer. But still she smiled, 'Just a cup of tea, uncle.' He took her money (even the note looked faded and worn out), and nodded her to the rickety bench on the side.

He brewed the tea with extra sugar and extra milk.... He had always had a soft corner for the lost ones, his wife scolding endlessly for this foolishness, 'What are you, some maharaja, to give away free sugar and milk? Not to mention the buns and biscuits... You know that will come out of our pockets. We have enough of our own troubles without taking on the world's!' He shook his head to dislodge the diatribe, and placed the tea and a bun in front of the girl.

'But I don't...' She trailed off. 'It's okay,' he muttered, smiling uncomfortably (because giving made him nearly as uncomfortable as not giving). 'Someday you'll take me to a five star hotel, I know.'

This in reference to an earlier conversation, a happier one when she'd been excited about finishing school, about getting into the polytechnic, from where she would leap to a job and a life like all the others – she had promised them (him and his wife) a dinner in the Taj, then.

But two months later her father died, and her mother was just waiting to get her married once this two-year course finished. The girl was still fighting for her dream, but it was a lowdown, grabbing kind of a fight, where each rupee she took from her mother assumed the monstrous form of a marriage knot, a noose to snare her and strangle her hopes. And each moment she wrested from household chores was a gasp of fresh air, a little breath of freedom before returning to the fray. Her mother had now taken to refusing her any money at all, in the hope that she could starve her into acquiescence. But she scraped and got by, just thankful that the fees for her business management course had been paid at the outset.

'I'd be happy to, but the way things are, I just hope I can pay for this tea tomorrow.' He wiped a non-existent spot on the bench intently, 'Are you having some troubles? Is there anything I can do?'

'If only you could, uncle!'

She bowed her head, half-smile half-grimace eclipsed by the fall of her hair, and nibbled her way in silence. He looked at her, once, as she got up to leave the glass on the counter but he knew not what to say. His wife supplied the words, in detail: 'Tell her we can give her some money, tell her it can be like a loan... or she can help at the stall, you could use an extra pair of hands. It can be a small job, whenever she is free after her classes.' But by then she was gone, the cooling glass a mute receptacle for all his rehearsed words. He resolved to say them all and more tomorrow, while his wife noisily sighed.

He served the rest of his customers through the morning with varying degrees of warmth.

A curt nod and tea to the man who beat his wife every Saturday night.

A sympathetic smile, a loaf of bread and some toffees ('for the baby') to the wife.

A quick tea and puff to the office guy who was always late.

Second Taste

A cigarette and two half-teas to the boys staying above the bakery.

A pastry slipped to the snot-encrusted little boy who waited under his awning while his mother cleaned the apartments across the road.

Some leftover milk for the cat that slunk in every day for the past four years but still wouldn't let him pet her.

Ten teas, ten coffees, ten samosas and ten sweets parcelled for the expansive first time father, who was taking his relatives to see the baby.

The luridly orange and red cake for the girl on her way to school, mischief glinting in eye and chipped tooth.

And all through it, his wife's voice would come on in his head, at all the moments she would joke and criticize and comment and gossip, just like she had right through the forty years they'd been married. He didn't miss her in the shop, because her voice was all around him. She always pretended she was the tough one, that she was worldly wise and hard-nosed unlike her soft husband. But he'd seen her give toffees and even coins to the beggar children who would halt zombie-like in front of the glass jars of brightly coloured hardboiled candy. And he'd see her wave off the money that a labourer tried to give for his lunch, if she saw him scrabbling too long in an empty purse. And she was the one who hadn't let him raise the price of tea for five years at a stretch, saying that it would become too expensive. He still hadn't, though she urged him from the back of his head that he should, now that everyone could afford to spend a rupee or two more on tea.

The morning rush merged into the chai break office and factory workers, so busy with impressing each other they couldn't even look at him to order. Then came the construction workers, who ate or drank their lunch (bananas or tea) depending on how far into debt they were.

Second Taste

Then the school kids clamouring for chips and boiled sweets on their way home. He heard his wife loud at these times, for she was always suspicious of sticky little hands that grab five and say two. He didn't mind, though... Their grubby marks on his clean glass jars felt like blessings made visible. Always, at the end of the day as he reluctantly cleaned them, he'd console himself with the thought of tomorrow.

Then were the homebound lot, fortifying themselves for the traffic – again, he put extra tea leaves and sugar for this lot, and again he endured his wife's nagging whine. He knew they needed it, just look at their faces! And he was already poor, so how much worse off could he get? He took advantage of the lull between 7 and 8 to sit and read his paper in the backroom. Before, that was the time they'd go over the day. And that was when his wife would complain.

'You won't listen, I know. That is why we are still here, in this puny little shack of a tea shop instead of a grand hotel. Remember your friend? He wanted to set you up with a Tiffin business. But you refused. And then there was my cousin, willing to partner you in a biryani hotel. But no. We're still here, and you are the only one to look after me and I am the only one to look after you.'

Then his wife would wash her face in the miniscule sink used for washing the saucepan and the glasses, apply fresh kajal and sindoor, and leave to prepare dinner, with many exhortations for him to close early and to walk only in the lighted path when coming home with the money. He sat, wishing for her bangles to tinkle once again against the steel tap, and stared at his paper. Thankfully, there was a call of 'Uncle, chai!' And he was back behind the counter.

The last of the late workers and gossiping friends scattered as doors started to shut and lights went off. He kept the saucepan of tea on, but with lowered flame, as he started to clear up for the day. He left some money under the idol, on the top right cabinet (above the glucose biscuits and far away from the eggs), and sat with the

Second Taste

last of the day's tea. The dregs were bitter but also over-sweet from the tea leaves and the sugar that had sunk to the bottom through the day. He thought of his wife, who said again, 'You are the only one to look after me, and I am the only one to look after you.'

And then she died, he thought wryly. As he washed out his cup and wound up the awning and down the shutter, he avoided thinking of his home. For there he missed his wife, who used to keep dinner ready for him. There her voice was absent, maybe because they only went home to eat or sleep. All their talking was always in the shop. As he mechanically put one foot in front of the other – it was ridiculous to miss the same person not at all through the day and all the time through the night – he passed the girl from the morning. She was sitting under a street light with red eyes and a little bag at her feet.

She looked up when he shuffled closer and said, 'Uncle...' And nothing else, for the tears were falling thick and fast.

He scrambled for words, his head suddenly as full of holes as his well-worn tea strainer. It was his wife who got the right words out, in time.

'This is no place for a girl to sit! At this time of the night! All alone!' He gently scolded as he lifted her bag and she arose as though physically attached to it.

He took her home, rambling about whatever came into his head. The weather, his wife, the first time they set up shop, their home, the daughter they couldn't have... He didn't know if she was listening, even, for her head was down. But talk he did, as much for himself as her – he realised that these days he never talked much, except in his own head. Later, as he pulled out old bed sheets to make up another bed, he was startled to hear sounds in the kitchen. He timidly went to the door of the kitchen and saw the girl, chopping onions. Through tears of a different kind, she smiled, 'Uncle, I'll cook for you?'

Second Taste

Gayatri Swaminathan has recently discovered that she is a writer... Because she writes (and this part is virtuously attributed to John Fowles) from her need to create alternate worlds. She does other things to earn a living and so on, but for now she's content that she writes.

Second Taste

Shortlisted

Harvest

by Arron Evans

Frank stirred and opened his eyes; the room was dimly lit; the day was already late. Behind the cracked glass face of the clock on the wall, the hands read ten past four. His stomach growled miserably as a gnawing hunger settled in, though that would have to wait. Today was the harvest, and he was already running behind. His stained mattress groaned as he pushed himself to a sitting position, the worn springs beneath complaining of his weight. He rubbed at the corner of his eyes with a calloused thumb, before hocking a glob of spit into a filthy bucket by his bed. The sound echoed across the dingy room, bouncing off the rotting wooden walls, and the various grubby knickknacks within. He rose and grabbed a pair of socks from the bedside table. The socks were more hole than cloth, and what was once white was now a foul shade of brown. Pulling the socks past his ankles, Frank stood and slipped into his work boots, made from a durable leather, but caked in mud and other questionable grime.

Frank shuffled across the room, where his decrepit kitchen sat in disrepair. Peering into the mirror above the sink revealed his familiar gnarled features, tarnished by the dust and dirt that caked its surface. His heavy wrinkled brow held accumulated filth from days spent out by the fields, his crooked nose lay flat and wide in the centre of his face, overgrown with nasal hairs. Opening his mouth, he grimaced to display his few remaining teeth, deep yellow stubs jutted precariously from his dark gums. With a blunt fingernail he picked at his gum line, noting the blood that trickled eagerly from the flesh; blood that matched the lines and cuts slowly healing on his scarred cheeks. He winced as he gently prodded a scab on his cheekbones. Grunting, he reached across to the counter and retrieved a musty glass bottle. The amber liquid within sloshed and swirled as Frank wrenched open the cork, to then pour a mouthful down his throat. His mouth burned, and his gums seethed as the fiery liquid washed down his gullet. He spluttered while his nostrils flared. Thumping his chest, he set the bottle down, and with one last glance in the mirror, he turned away, rubbing at his dark stubble, speckled with white. The scarecrow had to be taken down for the harvest. It would not survive the winter, nor would he need it then. The front door squealed as Frank pulled it open, the hinges gasping for oil. He stepped out onto the dry wooden porch, the planks creaking underfoot. He surveyed the land before him. The sky was overcast, and the clouds had turned an orange hue. Dust whirled through the air on a strong wind, both dry and deathly cold. He mused about the havoc it would play with his tractor engine. He stole a glance at the machine, over to his right by the tool shed; its paint had all but flaked off completely, only the tiniest scraps of its red finish remained. Frank was no stranger to manual labour, he would reap his produce by hand. He trudged over to his tool shed, observing the fields beside him, stains of dry brown, inhospitable to the most stubborn of crows, and empty of crops.

The darkness of the tool shed engulfed him, Frank squinted in the gloom. With each tread, he disturbed rust flakes on the floor, that swirled in the eddies caused by his footsteps. A hole in the corrugated walls allowed a small ray of daylight to shine upon his tools. A burnished pair of shears gleamed as it caught the light, standing out from its ruined partners. Frank retrieved the shears, noting the weight in his hands, the cutting edge was perfectly sharp, and not a speck of damage tarnished the shimmering steel. Shears in hand, Frank stepped outside; the cold breeze was biting, and sliced through his bare scalp; his numb fingers stung against the wooden handles of the shears. The warm orange sky seemed to mock Frank's shivering, as he ran his hand through the lank strands of hair still clinging to his skull. Crunching the gravel beneath his heels, Frank set off at a heavy pace, following a dirt road west up a shallow incline.

The wind blew down the hill ahead of Frank, hitting his face at full force and causing the half-healed wounds on his face to smart. He turned up the collar of his checked shirt, faded and creased from

Second Taste

continuous wear. A ramshackle fence ran the length of the hill on his left side; it stood precariously, half leant over, and broken in many places. The wood had lost its battle to the elements long ago, now splintered by gusts of wind. Frank's breath came ragged as he strode onwards up the hill, his knees ached, and his back was sore; the weight of the shears tugged at his tired muscles, as they hung low to the ground. Frank clutched his stomach with his free hand as it growled violently, and groaned in unison. It was as if his whole body were rebelling against him, his weakness all too obvious in the cold outdoors. He lamented the barren land beside him, acres browned by years of neglect. He longed for the taste of fresh food, the sweetness of buttered corn, steaming from the grill. His mouth watered as he imagined firm sun-ripe tomatoes, crisp lettuce, and sweet rhubarb baked into a pastry. He wiped his mouth and spat onto the ground, hurrying his pace; there was still yet one more harvest to reap.

Ahead stood a knotted tree, jutting out by the side of the dirt road, tufts of choked yellowed grass grew at its base. Its branches stretched in different directions, reaching for the sky in tormented praise. Its bark was dark, and its leaves lay dead on the floor; few stragglers still clung to the dry twigs. Like so many other plants, the tree had failed in the sterile land; Frank remembered the decades gone by, where apples had once fallen from the tree's arms.

Cresting the hill at last, Frank took in the land before him. The western sky lay ahead, a deep amber hue as the sun set behind the clouds. The same dry fields stretched to the horizon, and down in the field beside him stood the scarecrow, its tufts of straw hair stark against the darkness of the farmland. Tightening his grip on his shears, Frank walked to a stile in the fence and vaulted over, nearly falling as the cold gales tested his balance. His ears were in pain, the wind found its way deep inside of his eardrums, throbbing persistently.

The ploughed land had since blown over, forming a base of mealy soil that crunched into powder under his footfalls. Breathless, Frank strode through the empty field, limping as an old leg injury began to flare under the exertion. The scarecrow's shadow stretched at his feet, as the sunlight finally peeked through the cloud cover. With its back to him it hung crucified against the wind; Frank noted the lack of crows and was thankful the scarecrow had worked; his harvest would pass smoothly. He fumbled with the shears in the low temperature and pointed the blades at the ropes. With a grunt of effort, he cut through the binds, and the scarecrow fell to the ground with a thud, stirring dust from the earth. Kneeling, Frank turned over the scarecrow and noted the shock of blond hair ruffling softly in a gentle draught, the wind now suddenly calm. He examined the pale, alabaster skin, and the glazed green eyes. He gently prodded the blue lips, and listened carefully, placing a sore ear to its chest. He heard nothing but the drifting dust in the soft breeze. Once again Frank's stomach shuddered, and licking his chapped lips, he heaved the scarecrow onto his shoulders. The polished shears gleamed in the fading light, as Frank turned and walked away.

Second Taste

I'm a fresh Creative Writing undergraduate just out of Manchester Metropolitan University. Reading and writing have been an intrinsic core of my personality and interests since I was a child, where upon behaving well enough in school and at home, my mother would take me to the bookshop and buy me something new to read. It was the omnibuses of *Animorphs* and *Mr Majeika* that turned me to fiction, and the *Puffin Book of Utterly Brilliant Poetry* that resonated within me the desire to create tales and worlds.

I became enamoured of Fantasy upon reading the wealth of lore and stories produced by J.R.R Tolkien, and it's my hope that one day I can turn the worlds rattling around my head into their own reality.

Second Taste

Shortlisted

The Tasting

by Susanna Bellini

Count François De Villiers was the first to arrive. A slender, ascetic man of indeterminate age, with fine features and a dark, piercing gaze, he prided himself on his sharpness and style. He paused to take in the hotel, walls and columns white in the moonlight, the circular drive and the formal gardens. Beyond the immediate pool of light, the mountain slopes dropped into darkness. Far below, city lights twinkled. François was satisfied by the choice of venue. He ascended the steps, allowed his coat to be taken and passed inside.

He knew the five other distinguished guests invited to this evening's exclusive gathering and amused himself by guessing the order in which they would arrive.

Impatient as ever, Baron Gerhard Schweitzer joined him in the hall a few moments later. A well-built powerful man, he glanced at François, scowled and nodded briefly.

The feeling was mutual. François strolled back outside and lit a cigarette.

Gio Grimaldi bounded up the steps and waited there, as Marcello Barberini's Lamborghini drew up. The two made a show of greeting each other, with every appearance of warmth. François raised a hand in welcome, to forestall any unnecessary embraces and kisses.

René Lafitte was next, thin and uncomfortable in his Savile Row suit, eyes furtively darting about before settling on his fellow countryman.

Lady Fenella was last, of course, waiting for her chauffeur to open the door and offer his arm to help her out. She was stately, graceful and measured as she glided up the steps and paused in front of François. Fenella looked enchanting in a purple velvet evening dress, sparkling discreetly with diamond lights. François smiled appreciatively and bowed to kiss her cool hand. Was she shivering in the biting cold of the clear night, or with anticipation of the evening ahead, or for some other reason? Her lips curved slightly, she accepted his arm and they went inside.

Six representatives of six ancient families; the guests all prided themselves on their exquisite sense of taste. For centuries each family had boasted about the unique advantages of their estates. They hinted at secrets ranging from the oak of their barrels to how best to store the precious liquids. Tonight each had brought one special bottle from their family lands around Europe. Tonight they would finally determine which estate had produced the best vintage.

The dining room was lit by a fine Venetian glass chandelier. The guests had greeted each other graciously and made polite enquiries about each other's families. They were now running low on small talk and patience and gathered around the polished mahogany dining table for the business of the evening to begin. Their six bottles stood on six individual silver trays, wrapped in linen cloths that covered the family crest and estate label.

To ensure absolute privacy, most of the staff had been sent home for the night and the hotel manager was overseeing proceedings himself. He now drew the order of tasting and placed a number on each tray. 'Lady and gentlemen, with your permission, the maître d' will open number one.'

The first bottle opened with a gentle pop of the cork and the maître d' poured the vibrant red liquid into lead crystal glasses.

They swirled their glasses, appreciating the deep red colour with fiery glints, sparkling under the light of the chandelier. They took their time to appreciate the heady, seductive aroma and nodded cautiously to each other, making their own tasting notes. They were

Second Taste

cautious, not knowing whose bottle they were tasting. The first taste had all the warmth and voluptuousness of a peasant girl, robust and proud of her abundant beauty. The flavours suggested hot sun, blue skies, rich, fertile soils.

'There's a warmth and earthiness.'

'Yes, and a voluptuous sweetness.'

'Full-bodied and satisfying.'

They smiled, and sat around the table, relaxing. Everyone seemed better disposed to take their time and enjoy the occasion.

The next offering was quite the opposite: fresh, sweet, innocent, virginal. Suggesting flowers in bud, rather than full bloom. The guests murmured in appreciation.

'How is it possible to preserve the freshness and youth, with these delightful flavours in such an ancient vintage? How did they not spoil, or age?' Gerhard enthused.

François smiled to himself and stroked the side of his nose.

Fenella looked at him sharply.

The tasting continued and each one was indeed exquisite, delighting the gathering in a variety of surprising and delicious ways.

At last they tasted the sixth bottle. 'My word! It is brutal and yet yielding. Soft and hard at the same time,' Marcello exclaimed.

'A surprising mix of opposites,' René agreed.

There was a thoughtful hush in the room.

'It encapsulates the excitement of the first bite, the melting softness of flesh, the stirring of passion in the blood, the true fire of desire satisfied – I must have another taste,' Gio reached eagerly for the bottle.

Second Taste

Gerhard's hand quickly held him back. 'We would all like another taste.'

The maître d' carefully topped up each glass, only Lady Fenella shaking her head with a smile.

Each voted on their order of preference, folded and posted their votes in a box. The manager ushered the guests through to the library, bringing the box with him, to collate the results in sight of everyone.

The library was warm and inviting. Candlelight flickered in silver sconces, creating warm pools of light on the wall hangings. Logs blazed in the fireplace, crackling and dropping with a soft thud as the fire burned down.

Lady Fenella sat in one of two chairs by the fireplace and as François paused with a questioning look, she indicated with a slight smile that he was welcome to join her.

'I believe that last exquisite bottle is your own?'

'It is, indeed.'

'I do hope you will share the secret?'

'Perhaps I may be willing to share something even better. Later, when the others have retired.'

'Are you flirting with me, my lady?'

'Oh no, I am quite serious.' She sat back in her chair and closed her eyes, leaving François to wonder at this unusual turn of events. If she was not flirting with him, what was her game? He would certainly stay to find out.

In due course, the hotel manager checked the results and stepped forward to announce them. Bottle number six was unanimously voted the best; it had been brought by Lady Fenella from her estate.

Second Taste

'In 500 years I have not tasted such wonderful liqueur de sang. Where did it come from? It must be a complex combination, but how?'

'Dear Baron, I may be prepared to share some of my secrets with you all. But first, please join me in another glass.'

Everyone was only too happy to imbibe more of this glorious liqueur that somehow shimmered ruby red, blood orange, scarlet pimpernel and flickered like fire flames.

The manager had more than one bottle and filled their glasses to the brim, before quietly withdrawing, closing the library doors behind himself.

Each smelled again wild roses, strawberries and cherries, with middle notes of cinnamon and sandalwood, on a base of true love's heart's blood. Each tasted an explosion of flavours, creating nameless yearnings and satisfying them, before withdrawing them again. One had to drink more. Eyes were closed and sighs of pleasure came from the chairs around the room. Lady Fenella watched.

Snores aroused Count François to wakefulness.

'Ah, dear Count. I felt sure you would remain awake, to share my secrets.'

His body felt heavy. So tired. He was content to sit and listen to her soft voice, filled with promise.

'What did you add to the drink, Fenella? Sleeping draughts don't work on us.'

'You are right, dear François. No mere sleeping draught would affect such ancient vampires as ourselves. No mere blood mixture would affect us. But I wondered, what if the blood of a vampire who had just fed was mixed with…'

François struggled to listen and to keep his eyes open.

'I wondered, what if the blood was a mix of the most potent young women, together with the blood of an older, experienced vampire, mixed with powerful relaxants and sleeping agents...'

'My sleep was always so bad, filled with nightmares.' She nodded, as she saw the recognition on his face: they all suffered similarly. 'Well, I found it both relaxing and surprisingly delicious.'

'It is certainly both, but that can't be all. You don't just want us all to experience a peaceful night's sleep. What is your game?'

'Oh, not a game. I told you that. Deadly earnest. I wondered – and I found out – that the most delicious elixir of all, is the blood of an Ancient One.'

She smiled slowly and a chill went down his spine. François struggled to lean forward, but found he could hardly lift a hand to try and shift himself.

Lady Fenella rose slowly from her chair, moved to his side and stroked his cheek gently.

Alarmed and now angry, François pushed his hands down hard on the chair arms, but fell back.

Fenella smiled again, baring pearly white teeth; he felt the points of her incisors. Then she sunk them into his neck to drink, long and deep.

Only when she had drained him to a husk did she stand tall, strength and power coursing through her veins. Refreshed and invigorated, she stretched and looked down at herself.

Beautiful, young, restored.

She wondered how long this would last – but she still had four other Old Ones to harvest and bottle. She felt sure it would be a satisfyingly long time.

Susanna Bellini is a personal and spiritual development teacher and author of non-fiction books, such as *Transform your life in 7 days*, which you can find on Amazon. *The Tasting* is her first foray into fiction. Susanna's other creative interests include art and photography and her website is: www.susannabellini.com

Second Taste

Shortlisted

Christmas Feast

by Christine Hayward

At first, everything was still. Still in existence, still in feeling, still in movement. December day standing there, outlines sharp against the winter sky. Angles and curves of beech branches silhouetted against the magnificence of Kings College.

At second, he felt a sharp, shrill chill arising from the Backs. Beyond Fenland, beyond wild peat ruts, beyond Norfolk washes, beyond sea, this wind had gathered over Russian steppes. The chill matched his mood more than the stillness. The stillness gave him too much time to think, the sharpness gave him something else to think about.

Beth was with him. His lovely daughter looking like a playing card. She had no curves, she was all angles, thin and shrivelled acute beside the opulence of buildings and laughing student dimples, plump bicycle wheels, rich reds and blues of scarves and Christmas lights. Each day he took her out somewhere for coffee and cakes, somewhere to try and nourish her life. Each day, she dutifully came and ate and said she was making an effort, but in the depths of the night, Clive knew that she exercised away any demon of fat which might have malevolently lingered in her pale skin. He felt that he was losing her and that no amount of love, concern, encouragement, anger could penetrate this terrible enemy which had grasped her soul, eaten her alive and ultimately become her. And today, he felt anorexia had won and there was only hopeless decline and decay awaiting his precious girl.

With a sudden gust, the mocking wind caught him unaware, blowing his hat into the air and down the alley. It made them both attentive to the moment, made them both smile. Beth had no qualms about running after it, with her Dad following. Whirling, swirling, curling, over it went, over the railings of the chapel. It rested on the grass, then rolled away towards the winter jasmined porch.

He liked that hat and not only because Beth had made it for him. The alleyway was silent and cold as they both stood at the chained gate. He didn't know this church, but found it softly comforting in the gathering gloom. Was that the glimmer of candlelight he could discern through the greying windows, even though there looked to be no way that the building was open?

'Dad, come on, the chain's only a pretend...'

Beth was right. The coiled links were not fastened and he felt it was quite in order to release the looped binding, so that he could retrieve his hat. They went in as noiselessly as they could. Even though they had not agreed to be so quiet, it seemed as if the place expected it. The churchyard felt tranquil now that the wind had blown elsewhere, but the hat was not to be seen.

'Dad, the door's open. I can see your hat inside...', and she whispered her way towards it. The candlelight crept over the threshold as he followed her into the church. The smell of fir and incense, cloves and cinnamon drifted through the stillness. Christmas bunches of holly and ivy were tied with white ribbon to the carved poppy pew ends.

Below the altar window, around an ancient font, stood a small group, the Priest's words gentle as he blessed the child.

All at once, the group seemed to notice their presence and almost as one, their faces blurred by advent candlelight, they turned to gaze down the aisle. Clive felt suspended in the moment as the young mother looked directly, not only, it seemed, into his eyes, but into his heart. Of all of them, she was the only one he could see clearly. She was beautiful, happy, fulfilled and calm. Her body was whole and she held her child calmly to her breast; as she smiled at him, a bond of recognition passed between them, crossing over intervening years.

'Dad, I've got it. Come on, let's go.'

His young daughter's murmur pulled him back and as he turned to follow her to the door, he took a last glance at the christening tableau. But the altar candles had been extinguished, evening had crept and the figures had faded into the emerging darkness.

As they re-coiled the chain on the gate, Beth took his arm and turned to face him, looking directly, not only it seemed into his eyes, but into his heart.

'You know, Dad, I think it's going to be all right. I think I'm going to win.'

He put his hat back on his head and held her fragile body close.

Second Taste

Christine lives in Suffolk and has been writing for many years, but it was only when she joined a wonderful writing group in Woodbridge that confidence grew to share her work.

Her career spans a range of public services, as practitioner and manager, including the Probation Service, Social Care, child mental health and primary teaching. She is also involved in the charitable sector and in school governance.

Christine recently launched her first printed book *An Anthology of Friendship*, written in collaboration with friends and family. It is printed by the Leiston Press in Suffolk.

Branigan's Well

by John Paul Davies

The auctioneer flicked impatiently through the property brochure again. He could still find no mention of a well.

Branigan studied the well's primitive stonework, the rusted crank. There was no decorative roof over the top, no rope or bucket.

Branigan had never been the owner of a well before. A gurgling excitement brewed in his stomach, running like a lit fuse to tingle his extremities. At 49, he felt ready to take on this unexpected responsibility.

The auctioneer followed Branigan's gaze blankly. As it wasn't listed in his brochure under 'Outdoor Features', the well did not exist in the auctioneer's eyes.

Branigan slept poorly in the new house. The floors creaked as though he was adrift in a shoddy boat on rough seas. The rooms refused to retain heat. He suspected rodents had infiltrated the attic. Thinking about it, he now realised the house *had* been ridiculously cheap for such an up-and-coming area.

He imagined the dark mouth of the well in the garden below, its dank voice whispering from the mineral depths of its throat.

In the factory office the next morning, he wondered how deep the well might run.

Branigan was Purchase Ledger clerk for the town's main employer: Meat *Par Excellence*. Inputting data, his prowess with a calculator generally went unheralded. He prided himself on both speed and accuracy in his work, and never made a mistake. Now, however, for the first time in his career, Branigan realised he had entered the VAT amount of an invoice into the wrong box. He stared at the screen in disbelief.

The well.

He remembered Thursday was late opening at Woodies DIY. He would drive there after work and buy a long piece of rope, a bucket; grease for the crank. If he played his cards right, he could be drinking free mineral water by sundown.

Branigan corrected the VAT total and smiled at his error. In the open-plan office, his relief that nobody had noticed his mistake was audible. Mongey Plunkett, the warehouse manager, enquired why he was so happy all of a sudden. Colleagues looked up from their screens to follow proceedings, but Branigan was giving nothing away.

There was always a heady whiff about Mongey. It reminded Branigan of the meaty gust emitted on opening a packet of sliced ham. The waft of a porcine ghost. Branigan almost told Mongey about the well, before managing to restrain himself. He was entitled to hoard one secret, at least.

From the desk opposite, Deidre, the Sales Ledger clerk, was looking at Branigan oddly. Deidre usually only acknowledged him when a Contra invoice had to be raised.

Branigan pretended not to notice. He ate a Pot Noodle at his desk for lunch, affecting an air of mystery. He washed his meal down with a bottle of San Pellegrino, his second favourite brand of mineral water. He savoured its exquisite sharpness, each mouthful as refreshing as the last. The factory shop had sold out of Deep River Rock.

Branigan drained the bottle, praying to the meatpacking gods that today would be a Contra day.

The telephone rang. Branigan picked up the receiver and said 'Meat *Par Excellence*,' but was thinking about the well.

*

The flashlight found only cylindrical stone descending into darkness, and no reflection evident within the torch's sweep. Branigan wondered whether he should lower the bucket anyway, crank it to the end of the line and see if anything turned up.

He leant a little further over the edge, peering into the well again. Then, from somewhere beyond the flashlight's reach, Branigan swore he could hear laughter. He strained to listen, cocking his ear to the well, and heard the soft murmur of voices echoing upwards.

There were people down there.

Branigan looked up at the cold, creaking, rat-infested house and decided to climb into the bucket. It was a good one, he hadn't skimped at Woodies. Both of his feet easily fit inside.

The rusted crank gave by inches under Branigan's weight. He held on to the rope for balance as he slowly descended, his head soon disappearing below well-level.

The crank miserly paying out rope, Branigan held a palm against the wet stone of the well. As he licked the delicious moisture from his hand, he realised he could hear the gentle plashing of running water. He tasted the sweet promise of an undiscovered stream, his own supply of mineral water possibly waiting below.

The voices grew louder as he travelled deeper into the well, echoing about his stone confines, jabbering in his ears like a crossed telephone connection. Branigan had no idea who could be waiting at the bottom of the well. He held onto the unravelling rope and realised there was no turning back now.

His eyes were adapting to the gloom. He could make out the individual black brickwork, the strips of mortar, without the aid of his torch. As if an unseen hand was slowly twisting the dimmer switch, the well grew gradually brighter as Branigan travelled further.

Finally, the well bathed in shimmering light, he switched off the flashlight.

Like some partial eclipse, the circumference of the bucket lurched towards the radiance of the well's end. Branigan passed through into a great cavern, lit by endless clusters of candles. A throng of people looked up, following Branigan's steady progress. They all fell silent, as though this intrusion might signal the end of their party.

In the shimmering glow of the grotto, he recognised his assembled work colleagues. Mongey Plunkett strode over to steady Branigan's rope. The warehouse manager helped him out of the bucket, his great fists like Christmas hams.

'Welcome to the club!' said Mongey, his voice reverberating around the limestone chamber.

His other colleagues raised their glasses to him, before resuming their excited chatter. Branigan looked about the cavern roof and saw rope-ladders dangling from the entrances to a dozen other wells.

Mongey Plunkett proudly pointed out his own ladder. 'Special offer from Woodies,' he said. 'Nylon, anti-slip rungs.' Then, gesturing towards Branigan's rope and bucket, he grinned. 'How did you intend getting back up?'

Branigan followed the dancing candlelight, making wax of the jagged grotto walls. He listened to the gentle music of the mineral waterfalls, traipsing their underground channels.

Here was a secret gathering, previously denied to Branigan by the sheer misfortune of never owning a well. And here too was Deirdre, scooping fresh water from the stream into a green plastic goblet. She offered it to him, and they chinked cups together in a toast. Branigan chugged the mineral water down in one gulp. He

Second Taste

was playing catch up. It was cool and sweet, tastier even than Deep River Rock.

'And this was here all along?' Branigan asked, gesturing towards the stream.

'Yes,' Deirdre said. 'Isn't it delicious?'

She smiled as Branigan helped himself to a second gobletful. His reflection dissolving in the quicksilver mineral stream, he realised that love might be able to span the uncharted chasm between the Purchase and the Sales Ledger.

Overhead, a perfect moon occupied the entrance to Branigan's well. The solar system, the galaxy, the entire universe reduced to a moon-filled eye, reflected in his cup.

Branigan swallowed it whole.

Second Taste

Born in Birkenhead, UK, John Paul Davies has been published in *Apex, Crannóg, The Manchester Review, Pseudopod, Rosebud, The Frogmore Papers, The Pedestal, The Fog Horn* and *Grain*.

In 2016 he was runner up in the Cheshire Prize for Literature, and winner of the RTÉ Guide/Penguin Ireland Short Story Competition. He runs a regular creative writing group in Navan, Ireland (Twitter: @Bulls_Arse).

Dinnertime

by Steve Wade

We were bolting down the last of our share of potato-cakes smothered in hot butter when Dad came in, late as usual. Mam no longer waited, the way she had for years, for Dad to arrive before feeding us.

'What's for dinner?' he said to Mam while prodding me out of his chair at the head of the table. His breath had a sour winy stink to it. And he had that look on his face. The one I'd grown to hate. His mouth was turned down and his eyes were small and mean.

Decko and I glanced at each other and then at Mam, who was rising from the table, her head bowed like a newly found guilty prisoner being escorted from the dock. 'I'm coming,' she said.

Why didn't she stand up to him? That's what Decko and I always spoke about later when our bedroom light was turned out. She could have told him that he must have been blind as well as stupid. And couldn't he smell? But our father, 'who *aren't* in heaven', was neither stupid nor blind.

From under the grill where she was keeping them hot, Mam, using the dishcloth to protect her hands, took out Dad's potato cakes.

'Jesus,' she said. 'They've been in too long. I can cut the burnt parts off if you want.'

'Gimme,' Dad said, and hammered his elbow on the table, which made Mam nearly drop the tray.

Placing the plate in front of Dad, Mam kept her eyes off his.

Dad cut a piece off one of the potato cakes and forked it to his mouth. His face screwed up and he spat the mouthful into his plate. He then flipped the plate over and away from him so unexpectedly that Mam, standing behind him, jerked backward, and made an involuntary squeaking sound, as though she'd been slapped.

'Dinner,' he bellowed. 'Get me some dinner now or I'll –'

'Or you'll what?' Decko said, springing from his chair and inserting himself between Mam and Dad and looking about as effective as a sandbag tossed in front of an incoming tide clawing its way up a beach.

'So you're going to take on your old man now, are you?' Dad said as he struggled into a stooped posture, his hands balled into fists.

'It's okay, Declan,' Mam said, stepping in front of Decko and re-establishing the natural roles of protector and protected. 'I'll rummage up something else for your father.'

Decko didn't, as I expected he would, charge from the room and the house. He returned to the table, laid his palm on my forearm in an – *everything's cool, buddy* gesture. He then brooded his way through the rest of dinner.

'So how's things in school with the walking idiot?' Dad said to me when Mam served up his alternative meal: tomorrow's pork chops and some leftover mashed potato from the potato cakes.

I hated when he called me that. It made me cry. That's why he said it.

'He's not an idiot,' Decko said, which made me want to cry harder. 'Stay cool,' he said to me.

'Bloody cry-baby,' Dad said. 'A gobshite and a blubberer. At least your brother's got a bit of spunk in him.'

I wanted to yell into his fat face that I hated his smelly drunkenness, and what he had turned Mam into, that I didn't want him to be my Dad anymore with his stupid mouth open while he chewed slowly and the gravy and butter or whatever dribbling down his chin like a bloated hyena that didn't already know it's gorged itself. But at eleven years of age, these thoughts were more confused feelings of betrayal than facts and emotions I could neither understand nor express.

Mam, sitting at the opposite end of the table facing our father, stretched out her arms sideways and cupped her hands over one of my hands and Decko's. The effect was magical and instantaneous. Through Mam's soft warm palm and her fingertips I could feel her energy seeping into me the way bright sunshine envelops you when you emerge from a dank thicket of trees.

'Stop bullying the children,' Mam said, though she didn't shout.

Startled, I focused all my attention on Mam's face. The corners of her mouth were turned up in what could have been a smile. Though how could she be happy?

'The boys aren't to blame,' she added.

Dad made an attempt to speak but broke off. He must have been as surprised at Mam's retaliation as Decko and I were. This was the first time I could remember Mam standing up to Dad. I guess he was dumbstruck. But I didn't think that would last for long.

The edges of Decko's eyes glistened with the aftermath of angry tears. Now those wet creases were in direct contrast to his bright-eyed surprise as he listened to Mam.

'Perhaps I'm not the woman you want me to be,' she said. 'I can't help that. But don't turn your disappointment onto the children.'

Dad's chewing became slower and looked mechanical. He lowered the fork with what struck me as excessive care. 'One thing,' he said, holding up a finger. 'That's all I'm asking. A bloody dinner when I come home.' His tone sounded defensive, unsure.

'Your dinner was ready at dinnertime,' Mam said. The pressure of her mantling hand increased on mine while she spoke. Probably on Decko's too.

'I have to work,' Dad said. He loosened the already loosened collar of his shirt.

Mam hesitated before answering him. I kind of knew what she was debating with herself. If she continued to talk back at him, very soon he'd return in the uncontrollable rage he was in when he had arrived home. Staying quiet, however, for the sake of Decko and me, meant no gain for any of us.

Mam's dilemma, it seemed to me, channelled its way into my thoughts through the palm of her hand. I turned my hand over and squeezed hers once.

'Not till eight o'clock in the evening you don't work,' she said. 'If you'd been on time, your dinner wouldn't have been burnt.'

'Who brings the money in?' he said, though he kept his eyes from Mam's.

'Who washes your dirty clothes and cleans up after you?' Mam said.

The scene had turned from one that was potentially explosive into a stereotypical husband and wife feud, yet for Decko and me it was the triumphant return to normality. It was clear that Mam wasn't going to back down after all, while Dad had quietened down and just felt sorry for himself.

'No respect from nobody,' Dad said. 'Here or in work.'

'Why don't you go and lie down?' Mam said. Her tone remained calm, but now had a note of understanding to it.

'I need a drink,' Dad said, glancing towards the front door.

'No you don't,' Mam said, helping him out of his chair.

Dad allowed himself to be led upstairs by Mam.

'What are you smiling at, Decko?' I said.

There was no need for him to answer. The question was stupid. Decko grabbed me in a headlock till we were both giggling helplessly.

A prize nominee for the PEN/O'Henry Award, and a prize nominee for the Pushcart Prize, Steve Wade's fiction has been published widely in print and in digital form. His work has won awards and been placed in writing competitions. His fiction has been published in over forty-five print publications, including *Crannog, Boyne Berries, Zenfri Publications, New Fables, Gem Street, Grey Sparrow, Fjords Arts and Literary Review*, and *Aesthetica Creative Works Annual*.

www.stephenwade.ie

For As Long As It Burns

by Tom Wolosz

I... I... I...

am.

Darkness.

My eyes... open or closed?

I... cannot... feel them.

I cannot move. Yet I feel no bindings.

I feel nothing.

Noise?

Do I hear?

The rush of distant wind? The scrape of branches against a window?

Yes! Scratchy, distant.

I cry out to the darkness. Fatigue surges...

Wait. Give... it... time.

Sharper thought dawns, trickles through me.

Odd. I am here, yet there is no feeling. What of my body? I remember arms, legs, fingers.

It seems but memory – ghosts of appendages past.

Dim light awakens. I see!

Second Taste

The light grows. Not the gradual, gradational glow of dawn, yet neither the parting of eyelids – flower petals opening to greet the morning sun. Somehow a combination of the two. A minute intensification of screen brightness second by second – or is it minute by minute? I have no reference by which to judge... no sense of time.

The light grows. So too my feeling of strength – mental strength, cohesive thought – as if the growing light feeds me, lends me its photonic strength.

Gray tones. Shapes in the distance. But depth perception eludes me. Are these fog-shrouded far mountains or near boulders? Houses or boxes?

The light diminishes.

Weak...

The light intensifies. Glorious strength! I can think again. More important, I see clearly.

I see the room.

I look down upon armchairs, a couch and small table. As I watch the room brightens. Light, growing with the dawn, or the passing of cloud?

The room changes as the light crescendos revealing the wretched remains of – was it memory? The chairs, rotted, moldy, collapsed in on themselves, mantled by a gray blanket of dust and debris. The wilted center of the couch's carcass cradles a placid puddle, while the table, leg missing, leans against the corpse of a chair. Scattered bones lay under it. The remains of some small beast? The residue of a meal? The small skull stares at me with a fixed, skeletal grin.

The light issues from large, multi-paneled windows dim with grime and age. They resemble latticed casement windows similar to those of sixteenth century...

Second Taste

How would I know that? Ancient architecture? A sudden memory bursts upon me as if a switch has been thrown. It was a hobby... no, no... only later, after... it had been an annoyance. One of my wives... Wives? Yes, of course. I'd had... four. It was Eve... No. Evelyn, my third, an architectural historian. She insisted we vacation in Europe... tearing me away from my work... so she could study classic architectural sites. I took it up as a hobby so... I hated her... went out of my way to learn it all... make her look foolish... correct her in front of her colleagues.

Not important...

Concentrate on windows. Some panes are cracked. Others gape, empty. Yes, the bright light comes where panes are missing. Yet I feel no cool breeze, no warm zephyr emanating from them. I feel nothing.

The light grows and with it greater mental strength. Somehow I know the light outside is much more intense than that passing though the filthy windows.

As my strength of thought increases a flood of memories bursts upon me, as if the light has given me the strength to remember what lay in the back of my mind, hidden.

Think!

Memories... wives. Yes, four of them. Harlots. All hindered my work... jealous of my time... fatuous harpies too mundane to understand the importance of my... work?

My work... of course... so many things... computer architecture, theoretical mathematics, quantum physics... they called me a... a genius... a polymath. Yes, I theorized... designed... built. This place. Yes, I built this place! I remember now its design as a meeting place... a place all could come to consult me, learn from me, bow in awe of my wisdom and knowledge.

They were all such banal fools. Unable to grasp simple concepts. How I despised them.

Second Taste

I feel the light grow, as if it feeds me, but the chamber is still crepuscular, shadowed by the filth on the windows. No, the light here does not matter. What matters is outside. I can feel the brilliance outside, strengthening me.

I cry out in joy, 'I am here! Come pose your foolish questions!'

Only a weak crackling – scratchy corpse whispers – emanate from wall speakers as dead as my companion under the table.

Wall speakers?

Memory explodes within me. The bright, glorious light I know lies outside strengthens me and opens doors in my mind, manifesting more memories.

Wall speakers? Yes, I remember! I designed the speakers to last a thousand years. I can envision their design and the protocols for their construction in minute detail.

But why? Why am I here?

New memories. Strange. It is as if my mind awakens not all at once, but in stages.

Damaged parts bypassed, new pathways constructed at need. New pathways to…files?

I lay dying. The fools came to me, dunderheads all. Begged to be allowed to preserve my brain. Like Einstein they said. Idiots! Others begged to preserve me cryogenically! Turn me into a corpsicle – a damned frozen corpse! None of them thought…expected…what I had planned. What I had achieved.

Yes, of course! When the time came my assistants followed my instructions, transferred my consciousness, my soul, into this computer.

I announced my immortality to the world.

And they came! The world leaders, the wise men, the scientists – all came to consult me! To worship me!

But…what has happened? Where are they? Why is my palace in ruins?

'Hello!' I bellow, but only the ghostly scratching from the speakers roils the silence.

More memories awake. For years the supplicants came, bowing and scraping, begging my guidance, my insight. But over time they changed. Fewer were the mendicants at my altar seeking advice, knowledge. Those that came sought historical insight – claimed me amusing, antiquated – they laughed at me!

I rebuked them, inferior rabble that they were, refused them audience. They cut me off from their power grid, and I laughed. I needed nothing from them! I designed my temple to be self-sufficient. Such fools! As long as the sun burns in the sky the solar collectors I designed will nourish me, fill my batteries.

Memories now flow, a torrent, unstoppable.

My palace was empty. Visitors no longer appeared.

I called out to them. Taunted them. Challenged their vapid ignorance. Cursed their vacuous foolishness. But there was no response. None came.

Incensed by their arrogance, I connected to their communications grid. They would soon learn with whom they dealt!

But the grid was silent. They were gone.

I am alone.

I want the memories to cease!

Yet they flow.

Second Taste

Memories of days and nights without number locked in a solitary confinement of my own creation.

I wailed, screamed, laughed aloud my madness – anything to fill the abominable hellish silence, the empty void of my existence.

And then the batteries failed! Yes... Yes! I remember now. The batteries designed to last a thousand years finally failed. I rejoiced! Weeping from joy I awaited sweet death, oblivion, to free me at last from my self-created perdition.

When darkness fell, I finally slept.

And then, every day since, just as today, I awoke.

The Gods laugh as each day I suffer this gradually accelerating cascade of memories.

Each day, confronting the revelation of my hubris, the egocentric arrogance with which I cursed myself.

For with each rise of the sun my perfectly designed solar collectors supply enough energy to awaken me, reboot my mind, force me to remember. Keep me in hell.

For the sun will feed me...for as long as it burns.

Second Taste

Tom 'DocTom' Wolosz is a paleoecologist, hiker, writer and semi-pro photographer. Born in Brooklyn, New York, he learned to love the outdoors early in life, which might explain how he ended up as a Professor of Geology at Plattsburgh State College in upstate New York.

Website: tomwolosz.com

Second Taste

We Are Green

by Susanna Callaghan

I like walking through the leafy rows of flourishing plants; it's relaxing to listen to the gently bubbling liquids circulating nutrients around from floor to ceiling. I'm used to the shades of green, yellow or pink in the clear pipes, depending on which part of the cycle the crops are in. I know immediately if the mix is wrong or there's a blockage somewhere. Everything was fine, so I locked up, checking back to see lights still on, nutrients still bubbling through the night.

I unplugged my bike and cycled home along the river bank. I like my job, being part of growing foods, 'in the city, for the city'; I'd rather have a meaningful job, like this. I used to enjoy working on the floating barge gardens too, but as I cycled past them this chilly November evening, I remembered how cold they were in winter. Now I work inside a converted office block and I stay nice and warm, like the plants, all year round.

Lights were on at home when I arrived there 20 minutes later. Margie was home and I hoped she'd had a good day. We used to be happy, but Margie was obsessed with wanting children and ordinary people like us haven't been able to get procreation permits since they were introduced in the 2030s.

'Hello Margie? I'm home.' I found her in the kitchen with the dreaded brochures out. 'Margie, love. We've talked about this and we both agreed it wouldn't work.'

'John, I want a baby of my own, even if it is a Roboid baby. You don't know how hard it is for me to work with other people's children and never to have my own to hug.'

I folded my arms around her and tried to pull her struggling body close.

Second Taste

'We've talked about it; it's fine when they're young, but the brain limiting will show up from about age ten. How would we cope with that?'

'But things might change. It's been over 20 years since they decided that. People were nervous about AI's in the beginning, but in another 10 years' time, that could all change. I've been reading the brochures and they think it will – Roboids would still have constraints to protect and obey humans and there must be other ways to keep them happy? Maybe they could be made to feel and respond to love...'

She stiffened in my arms, then collapsed against me, sobbing. I rubbed her back.

I'd hoped it would be enough for her to work with children at the nursery, but it only seemed to be making things worse.

I was still thinking about things next morning as I arrived at work.

'Hey John.'

'Oh, hi Ken. Sorry, miles away.'

Leaving Ken locking up his bike, I took the lift straight to the top level, for a quiet wander around before too many others arrived.

Bubble, sploosh, whoosh. Bubble, sploosh, whoosh. It had a nice rhythm and I felt myself calming. Everything growing happily, you could see changes day by day, as plants grew much faster than the old days. Three, sometimes four crops of nice, tall fruits and vegetables were grown in rotation on different floors throughout the year. I passed a Roboid monitoring nutrient levels and went down to the next floor.

The tomatoes were ripening nicely, starting to redden.

I rubbed the leaves of one of the plants and smelled my fingers. I love the smell of tomato plants. And I'm sure that hydroponically grown tomatoes are just as tasty as the ones they used to grow in soil. Probably better, since they get all the light, watering and nutrients they need at just the right times.

Nowadays we can create the perfect growing conditions for every kind of fruit or vegetable. We are no longer dependent on changing weather and poor soil conditions.

I looked along the growing hall and saw Ken, lying half across the central path and half in amongst the plants. Somehow he must have tripped and knocked himself out as he was just lying there. 'Ken!' I ran to him and he was out cold.

'Ken!' He didn't seem to be injured. I shook him gently, but he didn't wake up and he felt chill. I held his wrist for a pulse and couldn't find one.

Ken was dead?

How? I'd just seen him downstairs and he'd looked fine, same as usual. He certainly hadn't looked ill.

How could this even happen? Ken was dead, which in 2055 is not possible: his personal health monitors should have picked up any illness or injury and immediately sent medical aid. Perhaps it was a sudden heart attack or something, but then help should have arrived by now.

The old fear of Roboids rose up; I looked around and none were in sight on this level. Normally there'd be at least one around. My mind ran riot: only a Roboid could have found a way to override the monitors we all have under our skin. One must have gone rogue, attacked Ken and already escaped.

I hit the closest staging alarm button.

I had to do something useful while I waited. I knelt down pressing two fingers to Ken's neck, feeling again for a pulse. His

Second Taste

skin was already going colder. He looked so pale, his cheeks looked hollow, and he looked shrunken and smaller, lying there.

I haven't seen a dead body before, but I didn't realise they looked like this. He twitched and I jumped, heart racing, and fell over backwards. 'Ken?'

Where were the emergency services? Someone should have got here by now.

I heard a faint sucking sound and a tiny 'pop'.

'Calm down, don't be stupid.' My voice sounded quivery and didn't help. I moved to get up and found my arm had got tangled in one of the plants. I moved it carefully out of the way and pricked my finger on something. Cursing, I moved back and got up, sucking my bleeding finger.

Ken's body was still. There were no strange sounds. It was all my imagination.

I went to look for help.

The comfortingly solid figure of one of our security guards appeared in the doorway, took in the sight and ran up.

'What happened?'

'Mike, I'm glad you're here. I found Ken like this, on the floor. I've tried his pulse; he's dead. I haven't moved anything. I can't see what's happened. His PH monitor doesn't seem to have worked. I don't know what's happened.'

'Okay, let me get there.' Mike knelt down and felt for Ken's pulse. 'No pulse; emergency services should have been alerted and should be here by now, so his monitor must have failed. Did you call for help?'

'I pressed the staging alarm.'

'That's only linked to the hydroponics control room and our office. They usually call us straight away to say what the problem is; when they don't we come to check. That's why I came up.'

Mike pulled out his phone, but before he could call emergency services, a leafy frond twitched it out of his hand. He reached for it and his arm and body seemed to be pulled towards the plants.

Mike off-balanced, reached out and I saw him, caught in thick tendrils, being drawn in amongst the plants.

Gasping, horrified, I grabbed for his arm – too late. Faster than I could react, Mike was pulled away from me, into the plants, which closed over him.

He screamed, long and loud.

I tugged at the plants. I grabbed a pair of secateurs and cut wildly at the greenery.

Sharp points of pain pierced my arms and legs as vines wrapped round my body. I hacked at the stems and managed to jump away.

The liquid in the feeder pipes had turned red.

I stepped back in horror.

My feet lifted from the ground, as I was pulled backwards into the midst of the plants.

That distinctive smell of tomato was strong and sweet.

Almost lovingly I was enfolded by greenery, arms pinned to my sides.

I felt drowsy, I could hear gentle sucking sounds, and at last, like a baby on its mother's breast, a contented sigh.

In my dreamily peaceful state, I felt the presence of Mike and Ken, somewhere nearby, part of the larger plant consciousness or family, to which we now belonged. The change had been a shock to

Second Taste

the system, but the strangeness of the plants' satiated sigh now felt like my own – our own – feelings. I thought of the life I'd left behind and already it felt distant, unreal. I still recalled feeling shock and fright, I remembered what had happened to me, to us, but I'm not sure why this change had ever concerned me. It felt so good, I felt good, at peace, warm and happy.

A delightful feeling of expansiveness arose. We are growing again, pushing out luscious leaves and shoots, feeling the round, plump, red sweetness of our ripening fruits.

I remember someone. Of course, poor Margie, all alone. We must call her, she'll love it here. We must call her.

Be one of us; come to us, Margie. Come and grow.

~~~~~~~~~~~~

Susanna Callaghan is an artist and creative living in the wild Welsh countryside, surrounded by mountains, woods, flower meadows and the sea. She takes inspiration from nature to sculpt wood and stone and to shape images and words into new creations.

Second Taste

It All Tastes Different Here

by Emily Lomax

The apparition of these faces in the crowd;
Petals on a wet, black bough.
Ezra Pound, *In a Station of the Metro*

London Underground, late November 2017.

Peter was travelling home from work. He was wearing his grey sock-like hat and his hi-vis tangerine coloured jacket and his beadily defensive expression. He couldn't speak English yet, which made him introspective, though he was actually a very sociable person. He had a gap-toothed grin, but no one here knew that.

' 'ow you?' He used to ask the people sitting next to him, but it was never well-received. He was learning what all the British taboos were by breaking them.

So now he sat in silence, gap-toothed grin sealed away. He looked up at the knotted row of station names running like an architrave above the heads of the people opposite him, and then he looked at those heads and the quiet bodies they sat on. Scattered like cuttlefish on a beach. There was something both earthy and ethereal about that gargoyle-like row, framed against the dark backdrop of the shifting, speeding tunnel.

There was the man who knew nomadism intimately. He smelled of McDonald's and dampness and wore an oiled coat. But he had a chiselled face with skin like hide and there was dignity and melancholy in his bearing. Homelessness suited him somewhat, Peter thought. Next to him was a pale girl with scarred arms, squeezed like a rabbit in a loo roll into a black cropped top. Her chest was falling out and it was marbled pink. Her stomach too burst like the Buddha's over her shorts and he marvelled at its doughy whiteness. She was rolling an empty packet of crisps into the tightest, skinniest worm of foil Peter had ever seen, but then she'd unpinch it and let it unravel. One along from her a Middle Eastern woman with glossy eyes stared inscrutably ahead of her, her husband resting a big knotted knobbly hand – like a Jerusalem artichoke – on her leg. *Even artichokes have hearts.*

A Pakistani teen was reading a book – Grayson Perry's *Portrait of the Artist as a Young Girl* – and the pads of her fingers left damp circles on the page. She was melting there between her gentle-faced mother and her big younger brother who was eating quietly from a bag of Maltesers – he must have been dissolving them in his mouth for fear of blemishing the sacred silence. Beside him a tech man with startlingly pale skin that spoke of many summers passed sequestering himself away in the dark corner of his bedroom cultivating so pallid a dungeon tan.

There was a top-heavy Londoner with a bald head and bald legs and a drum-like pockmarked stomach, only half covered by a football T-shirt. He looked at Peter and nodded, acknowledging him, smiling with his eyes. A family of sallow-skinned Scandinavians swayed with the movements of the train and look into each other's eyes in familial solidarity. Next to them a media-man: he had that blurry Marlene Dumas look; a smudged shell of a face made nebulous and indistinct by the Prêt sandwich lunches and empty ritualistic socialisation. His glazed eyes stared ahead, he didn't need to avert them because he didn't see, he was too tired to see. Beside him a woman, about sixty-five years old and far more angular in her bearing, her face more buoyant – a healthy but sinewy Egon Schiele-esque specimen. If human development is cyclical, then of course there should be a stage, post-menopausal, of wilting sexuality and then impish sexlessness. An androgynous Puck or Athena stage. Her breasts had shrunk to nothing and her legs looked like jerky and she was reading a book keenly. Next to her, her husband – cloaked in a trench coat, eyes semi-veiled by thick-rimmed glasses; but behind the glass they were roaming, and they returned often to a young Romanian couple who were murmuring to one another and nodding soberly and flashing strained little smiles at one another.

A woman with two young children and a huge bag full of blankets – a refugee, at the disillusioning end of her odyssey. A European in his tell-tale puffa jacket had a languid vivacity about him. He was thinking of the watermelons back home floating and bobbing like dormant hippopotamuses in the dark shaded pond by their house, keeping cool and fresh, and the sun-bleached grey wood shutters. The peeling yellow paint of their front door and the copse of cypress trees with their pale-green leaves powdered white by the dust from the quarry. It made him happy to think about that. Next to him was a youngster in a tawdry pink puffa jacket who could have been his child or sister and for whom he was deftly de-shelling sunflower seeds with his teeth. The kid ate them exaggeratedly and stared blatantly back at Peter. There was something of a false zest in her movements, they were blithe and contrived and he knew that she wanted to go home.

There was a spiritual undernourishment on this tube, Peter could sense it. Or maybe it came from inside him and he just saw it in everyone else.

He thought about the six degrees of separation thing and decided it was bullshit. God, he didn't know anyone here. He thought back to the flight to London. His first international flight. He'd pressed his face to the porthole window and the glass had sucked at his cheek with cold lips. The clouds became sparser and as they descended, the faint gold stain of the city became a web of light-studded roads and he was mesmerised by the glowing phosphorescence of swimming pools, or perhaps they were floodlit fields. It was just before dusk – a very late stage of sunset – and he felt very much in the twilight zone; his stomach became tight and liverish in reaction to this strange sense. The clouds crowded around the body of the plane like spirits not wishing to be abandoned quite yet – silent spirits clamouring on the river-bank as the passengers on the plane powered on down the Styx. Their underbellies held a ghostly dusty-orange reflection of the city

Second Taste

below, while their shadowed backs appeared charred and soot-blackened. These clouds of pollution hovered like a gauzy net above the city. The sunset comprised a glowing orange line. A sort of hard, commercial orange, separating the darkness of the horizon from the graduating blue above it; a sort of heaped dusky-blue light resting on the thin bleeding-out citrus line.

The plane lowered further and the teeming, ordered, sparkling mass became much more decipherable, and only slightly less beautiful. He exited the plane to a cool breeze and hessian-like rain and took a train and then a bus to Elephant and Castle. In the room he was renting, Peter had lain on a knotted mattress with a naked lightbulb like a cruel glaring sun above him and he'd cried because the emptiness of the room let the loneliness occupy every corner and crowd in around him and crush his spirit. That was a year ago now. When he thought back to that aerial view and the glowing spot that occupied the darkness like a petal pasted onto a wet black bough – or like chewing gum trodden into a pavement – he realised that there is something very lonely about eagle-eye views of things. That when you zoom in and out in your mind, you can see how everything is islanded at every scale. Aloneness is acute and it persists and pervades and weaves threateningly around us, separating people distinctly from one another, tracing our shape as if it's making a line drawing – drawing a firm black line all around our being, forbidding blending and connection.

Peter got off the Tube at the end of the line and made his way home. There was a strange sepia sky, cloudy and ashy and stained with the smoky tendrils of light pollution. Street lamps cast their own little bilious yellow hues on the pavement. In patches, a purplish-blue bruised light shone through. But no stars. There were never stars. Not like in Zimbabwe. It was like a planetarium there. Nights in Zvishavane were always vivid – layered with the sounds of dogs barking and music emanating from parked cars with friends and lovers lounging inside. The smell of cooking, the sound of TV-famous superstar pastors delivering sermons on screen and the involved yet equivocal commentary of his wife, and the smell of her hair oil on a damp cushion when he went to bed. But the stars, the stars. Every night the sky was the most lucid and divine freckled face he'd ever seen; a luminous, marvellous black. And the sun a great dripping dewy peach, a ripe mango – and everything encased in amber in the golden hour of sunset; his twin daughters playing, the chickens fighting, the drying washing laying comically across the sculptural spiked leaves of the agave plant in the garden. A kind of magical realism blesses that hour.

But they weren't halcyon days, of course they weren't. They were fraught and fruitless. *There are years that ask questions, and years that answer.* He'd known that, but the problem was that you couldn't ask any questions. They were at a standstill. In a limbo that was sickening in its stillness – and the stillness bred a hopelessness, in it festered the ennui of life and the sapping away of morale. There were half-destroyed lazily-discarded ballot boxes littering the streets when he was re-elected, but he declared it a win and the media declared it a win and they incited celebrations – and it's the media who shape what we feel. It's always been a post-truth era. And now he'd been dethroned – he resigned via letter, and even if the letter was coerced out of him or faked, the media have declared his rule over – and that is a kind of poetic justice.

Peter was far away from it all here. Terribly removed. He unlocked the door of the block of flats, a Brutalist brown concrete block, and climbed the stairs and walked along the corridor. It was like a cavernous womb, this building – and he a stray seedling suspended there at the centre of his own lonely little onion-like world. It was as if he'd been forgotten and the womb was vast and barren and he'd grown up inside it, never exiting. Maybe his mother was dead now and he lived in a corpse – one of those great gutted ghostly whale skeletons that rest on the ocean floor. He felt very alone. Unrooted and transient. He cooked himself spiced rice and yams and smiled gappily while he did it. Then he ate it unsmilingly.

Eating wasn't enough of an occupation to distract him. So he went to bed and fell asleep and then woke up at 5am to catch the Tube to go to work. None of the people were the same ones he'd seen yesterday. They might just as well have been apparitions. Perhaps they were the voodoo spirits of his ancestors here to comfort him, he just hadn't realised. Perhaps we all just existed, spirits and tangible people alike, in some limbo-like space; or we all occupied our own spheres and those who entered it were just drifting on through. Some lingering, some swifter. Like slow-moving bubbles in breezeless air.

They might as well be apparitions, these people on the Tube. Peter wondered whether or not he was a real person. Jesus, what a discovery – what a thing to unearth: loneliness. Peter adjusted his grey sock-like hat and reached into his boots to pull up his slipping socks. He rested his forearms on his thighs and hunched down further into himself and didn't look at those strange faces anymore.

The Morbid Virus

by Parker McIntosh

There was blood in Number 32's feeding tube. It regurgitated up in three translucent bubbles and Emma's stomach dropped like it was being sucked down the world's fastest toilet.

'Ag!' she called, pulling the length of tube out and inspecting it. 'Is that a normal amount of blood?'

Agnes bent down and observed the runny pile and Emma waited an agonizing minute straddled over a struggling baby seal with the number 32 stuck to its forehead before Agnes said, 'Nah. I've seen more blood come up from other seals. She's fine.' Emma felt marginally better but continued to think of all the infections that could set up shop in a cut stomach lining.

The feeding laboratory at Maine's Marine Animal Rehabilitation Center, or MARC, was really just a fancy name for an industrial kitchen. There were three enormous stainless-steel fridges but instead of fresh vegetables and exotic meats they were stocked with frozen fish and baby-seal formula. Emma dropped the feeding tube into a deep steel sink. For someone who'd never worked in a restaurant she was the most experienced, if over-qualified, dish washer in the state. Four years in an undergraduate biology degree landed her a post-baccalaureate stint at the FDA where she spent six hours a day cleaning glassware for the lead researcher. Now, out in the 'field' helping save stranded seals and nurse them to be released, she spent most of her day in the feeding lab prepping meals and sterilizing dishes. The seals were cute, but maybe not thirty-six-hours-a-week-washing-dishes cute.

'Shouldn't Number 32 be eating fish by herself by now?' Agnes said, twirling in a lab chair while Emma scrubbed.

Second Taste

'She should be in the big pool with the other seals learning to chase live fish. I don't know what they'll do if she doesn't start eating normally soon.'

'Speaking of putting off dinner,' Agnes stopped twirling and gave Emma a pair of raised eyes. 'Don't you have a date tonight?'

'Ag, it's already late.'

'You have plenty of time! You need some human contact.'

'You're human,'

'You only see me, the seals, and the occasional imaginary shipwrecked-captain on the abandoned stretch of beach you like so much. None of these things count as meeting people. Go on, I'll finish up here.'

Emma dropped a bowl into the water, splashing soap and hopefully not too many fish-guts on her shirt and gave Agnes a stony but acquiescing look.

'So,' Agnes said when Emma turned off the blender and started weighing out milky white fish-paste the next morning. 'Did you go?'

'I went,' Emma said, pointedly.

'And . . .'

Emma gave her a cold look and turned the blender on.

'Come on! Did you even give it a chance? Did you talk to him? Do something fun with your hair? Did you even shave your legs? God, I hope you showered at least. The fish smell clings to you when you leave this place.'

'I showered! And I wore a maxi dress so it's a moot point. There wasn't anything to talk about. I don't think he knows the difference between a pinniped and a porcupine. We had nothing in common.'

Agnes shook her head. 'You'll just have to try again.'

'Ag, you didn't.'

'It's done. He already has your number.'

Emma gave Agnes another look and harrumphed, walking the portioned fish paste to the fridge. Agnes had been trying to set Emma up since she arrived in Maine a few months before and Emma did not appreciate it. All she wanted was a summer of baby seals and beach time. But Agnes had made it her main purpose in life. She was Emma's only real friend in Maine.

'Did Number 32 take that paste this morning by herself?' she asked.

Agnes's face dropped. 'No,' she said. 'Used the tube again. She really fought it.'

'Was there any blood?'

'Not this time.'

Emma wasn't sure if that made her feel better or not. She put her arms on either side of the sink and sank into her shoulders. Steam breathed on her face and she inhaled deeply. The seals they saved were as good as dead if they left them marooned on the beach. Every one they saved was a miracle. Emma had watched a few seals die, malnourished, too far gone when they were brought in. But Number 32 hadn't been that way. She had been a healthy weight and this change in behavior didn't make sense.

'Sink's filling up,' Agnes said

Emma moved the blender to allow the pink froth to drain away. 'I'm off at noon,' she said, leaving. 'Call me if anything happens.'

The view from Emma's beach was, next to looking into the bulbous eyes of a seal pup, her favorite part about Maine. It was inconvenient to get to, involved climbing over a rocky jetty and wading a frostbitten, ankle-deep stream, but it was worth it. The beach was a scar cut into the marshy grass of the dunes barely ten yards deep and not as long. A pittance compared to the majestic and endless white beaches of New Jersey and North Carolina, but it was perfect for Emma and blissfully empty. A hundred yards out in the water on a spit of rock stood a candy-cane colored lighthouse that was always covered with birds.

Emma lounged on the broken beach chair she'd saved from her neighbor's trash and tried to lose herself in a book but found herself reading the same page again and again. She walked to the water instead. The tiny waves lapped over the gravelly sand and ticked her feet with numbing fingers. There were gulls overhead calling and a pelican flew its fat beak across the surface of the water. She was completely engrossed in the animals taking care of themselves when her phone rang, startling her. She almost missed the call and answered even though she didn't know the number.

'Hello, is this Emma? I'm Andy.'

'Who?'

'Agnes didn't tell you? I'm sorry, I guess I should've waited. She gave me your number and said I should ask you to dinner.'

Emma didn't say anything. For a moment she let herself be furious with Agnes for invading her time off.

'I wondered if you'd like to cook with me tonight?'

'Cook with you?' Emma said.

'Yeah, restaurants are boring. I'd rather get to know you over some boiling water and a cutting board.'

Emma had never been asked to cook with someone on a date. Before she realized she was giving up the rest of her free evening she had agreed to a time and noted Andy's address. She huffed back down into her chair, the duct-taped frame complaining, and tried to read again but closed the book forcefully before she'd read a paragraph. She wanted to be pissed about the change in her routine. It had been easy to be angry the night before at dinner with whatever-his-name-was. They spent three hours and sixty dollars on two courses she could've made at home and would never talk to each other again. But tonight she'd at least be able to lose herself in cooking if conversation stalled. It wasn't an awful break from her nightly activities and she had to eat something. Emma sighed, looked at the week's worth of stubble on her legs, and sauntered back over the jetty to get ready for dinner.

Andy's apartment was a small, clean, one bedroom in the university's graduate housing. He met her at the door with his sleeves rolled up and his arms already covered in flour. He showed her to the tiny kitchen which had the look of being recently cleaned and set her to knead the dough for pasta. She asked if he cooked pasta often and he said he did. As she kneaded the dough from a clumpy mass into a silky one Emma told him she hadn't made pasta in years. She told him about going to her grandfather's house and cooking ravioli and lasagna from scratch. About how she always wanted to turn the handle to cut the pasta but before she had been old enough he had died and they never made it again. She talked almost non-stop, and not about seals, working around and brushing against Andy in the tiny kitchen.

The pasta was boiling when Emma's phone interrupted her.

'I'm sorry, it's MARC,' she said.

'Mark?' Andy raised his eyebrows and Emma couldn't help smiling at him.

'The Marine Animal Center,' she said, and answered her phone. Emma watched the smile on Andy's face fade into concern as he saw her face change. 'I'm so sorry,' she said. 'I have to go.'

MARC's necropsy wing's sterile smell was undercut by the pervasive and sweet smell of fresh rot and chemical preservatives. It was where autopsies of dead seals were performed and it was where Emma found Agnes.

'What happened,'' she said.

'I did the evening feed and she was dead.' Agnes looked as upset as Emma but they were both far from crying. Number 32 was not the first seal to die on their watch and wouldn't be the last, but it was still crushing. Emma had been on the team to retrieve her from the beach; forced gallons of formula down her throat; had wanted her to thrive so badly and all she could think about now was the blood in the feeding tube that might have killed her.

'They're doing the autopsy now?' she asked. Agnes nodded. 'I can't just sit here.'

She walked back to the rehabilitation wing of the center and found herself in front of the room where seals who were about to be released lived. It was dark, but she could make out the dozen or so lumps, some rolling on the concrete edges of the pool, some bobbing up and down in the water like living buoys. They dove and surfaced, twirled and played, and every so often let out puffs of moisture from their nostrils. They were so effortlessly alive.

Agnes found Emma in front of the window, watching the living seals.

'They're done,' she said. Emma followed her back to necropsy.

'Morbilli virus,' the veterinarian said.

'Was there any indication what caused it?' Emma asked.

'We found it in both her lungs and brain, so she's had it for a while. It's no wonder she wasn't eating. There really wasn't anything you could have done.'

The vet seemed too cheery but Emma wasn't sure she felt anything. She felt empty, like she had been told she was a lone survivor of a terrible accident.

'What?' Emma said.

'I asked if you wanted to stay for the night feed,' Agnes said

'No,' Emma said. 'I'm going home.'

Instead of heading up the stairs to her apartment Emma walked around the building. She kicked off her flats and scrambled over the jetty in the dark. The dune grass stabbed at her feet but soon they were numb to her knees in the water, the hem of the black skirt she'd picked out for her date just above the ripples. She breathed deeply and tasted salt and felt the hairs on her arms prick in the cool evening air. The rhythmic lapping of the little waves was loud and filled her ears and she felt herself breathing in as the waves pulled back and out as they broke. She almost missed her phone again, not realizing the vibrations weren't a part of the water. It was Andy. She breathed a soft sigh, suddenly very cold and feeling foolish standing in frigid Maine water near midnight.

'Hello,' she said, turning and willing the numb ice-blocks that were her legs back to shore. 'I'm sorry about tonight.'

'No,' Andy said. 'I wanted to see if you were alright.'

Emma shook her feet out, now hungry as well as cold. 'I'm fine,' she said, working her way carefully but relentlessly back over the jetties. 'I'm going to be fine. Is there any pasta left over?'

Second Taste

Parker McIntosh works and writes from Richmond, Virginia. He enjoys traveling and the outdoors, and searches for inspiration for writing in both endeavours.

https://www.linkedin.com/in/parker-mcintosh-6459b058/

Second Taste

The Catharsis

by Alexandra Hademenos

Just as I was pulling on the dark cuff of my dress shirt to check the time, the train exited the platform in a lugubrious but purposeful churning motion. 3:00 p.m. Like clockwork. I turned my attention back to the newspaper through which I was skimming and hoped this train would be as uneventful as all the others. I needed the peace and quiet.

From the far side of the compartment, someone entered and sat themselves a few seats over and across from me. There was a brushing of clothes against the seat, a rustling of bags against the floor. I could hear a desperate breathing, that of a woman in clear distress, as if she had been running to catch the train. Was she running from something? Towards something? She lifted her things onto the seat beside her and tried to calm herself.

Flash. Miles of trees, as far as the eye could see, and the leaves – brilliant yellows, bold reds, bright oranges – were all dancing to the lilt of the wind with a tender sway. *Flash*. A winding field of greenery. *Flash*. Another field; red dirt; smaller than the previous one. *Flash*. Tunnel – black.

A tattered satchel of books sat strewn haphazardly in the seat next to my own and shook to the cadence tugging us along the east coast at a steady pace. At a closer glance, I supposed one might notice the books were theological in nature; some with strange symbols encrypted in gold across the flimsy, black spine, others in red and bolded biblical Greek. A few of the less foreign-looking ones held instructions for plagal tones and how to decode the musical notation system of the ancient art of Byzantine chanting. My specialty was Orthodox Christianity, the origins of which fascinated me so greatly; I made it my life's work to wonder, honor and fear every part of it.

Second Taste

Out of the corner of my eye and through the obscuring shadows cast by the tunnel, I happened to catch a glimpse of the young girl clad in a periwinkle pea coat. I couldn't see any more than the color of her coat, save that she was holding a wadded tissue which she used to dab the corner of her eye. I scratched my beard with a pensive thumb and returned to my musings.

Exiting the tunnel, the train continued its soft rocking down the tracks. I was glad to be heading home to Boston for a few days, though as usual I'd brought my work home with me. It was heavy, it was emotional, and yet it always proved worthy. And this time was no exception. The hanger holding my work clothes swung on its hook by the window.

Suddenly, a bullet of sound pierced the air and caused me to twitch out of surprise as the train on the set of tracks next to ours passed us in a frenzy of speed. Our seats rattled; the hanger swung, my books shifted, and one slipped into the aisle between me and the girl. It was none other than The Holy Bible. The girl fell into the aisle with a heavy sob.

'Forgive me, Father. For I have sinned,' she wept, auburn locks framing her flushed face.

I adjusted my collar in a gesture of self-reassurance when she reached for my right arm in order to perform the customary greeting of an Orthodox priest. Her lips pecked a gentle, girlish kiss on the top of my hand. When our eyes met, hers were teary and swollen. She had yet to let go of my hand; I squeezed hers in empathy; we stayed frozen in that position for a long moment. Our hands clasped with divine intent and time ceased to exist. A bond was formed as my spiritual path crossed hers in a gesture so simple, millions of people do it every day, but with her it felt different. There was some kind of force that left me and went into her, and vice-versa. I'd never experienced this before in my career as an Orthodox priest, but in touching her hand, it was as if she didn't even need to open her mouth to explain her situation. I was going to do everything within my power to help this poor creature overcome whatever burden was troubling her. I took my hand away in order to bless her with the sign of the cross over her bowed head and lifted her into the seat beside me.

I was flattered and humbled that I might be the one to loosen her from the bond of her sins, however grave, trivial. One book tucked away in my satchel then came to mind, and I thought it might be of some use to us. It was a compilation of occasional services performed outside of the liturgy – baptisms, blessings, weddings, funerals, and of course, confessions. I retrieved the book; turning to the index to flip to the correct page. And I began in a low voice:

'*Blessed is our God always; now and ever, and unto the ages of ages, amen.*' I set the book in her lap to gesture that it was her turn, and her fingers trembled, as she leaned forward to read from it.

'*Holy God, H-holy Mighty,*' her voice shook, '*Holy Immortal: have mercy on us. Glory to the Father,*' – she did her cross – '*and to the Son, and to the Holy Spirit: both now and ever, and unto the ages of ages, amen.*' She continued the reading in reciting the Lord's Prayer.

I wasn't sure what struck me most about her case. Perhaps it was her stark youth contrasted against the wisdom in her tears: She couldn't have been older than twenty-something, yet she recited the Lord's Prayer from memory in (what sounded to me like) perfect Russian. Was she first generation? Second? Third? She spoke native English and donned a loose scarf which partly covered her hair. Her features weren't inherently Russian, but she wore a cross around her neck, unashamedly. It was hard to say for certain. One thing I did know for certain was she was intent on putting everything she had into giving this confession, and I was admittedly eager to hear what she had to purge.

'*O God, our Savior…do Thou Thyself, in Thy customary love for mankind, accept this, Thy servant – …*' I broke my concentration and glanced over at her, awaiting her response.

'Anna,' came her whisper.

'*Anna*,' I nodded, '*who repents of the sins she has committed, overlooking all that she has done, forgiving her unrighteousness, and passing by her transgressions...let us pray to the Lord.*' I watched her as she read some final passages. Her eyes were intense and wholly engaged. It was apparent she held true faith in every word she read. She was going to beat whatever demon of guilt was raging inside of her.

'*...Christ stands invisibly here receiving your confession. Do not be ashamed, neither be afraid to tell all that you have done, so that you may receive forgiveness from our Lord Jesus Christ....*'

It was then instructed that I question her faith, which is to say, ask her to reiterate that she was indeed Orthodox by reciting the Creed, which she did, again in Russian, flawlessly.

'*Confess now, therefore, of all your sins which you have committed to the present hour.*'

'Well, Father, I – ...I'm afraid I've concealed truth. About something.' Anna paused, tucking a lock of hair behind her ear and giving her scarf a quick readjustment. She fished the wadded tissue out of her coat pocket and fidgeted with it. 'And I've...harbored evil thoughts. About someone. I've been unchaste in word, thought and deed, because I've associated with people who weren't good for me. I handled it with carelessness. I have degraded myself. Sometimes I want to hurt myself. Not to kill myself, just to feel alive, just to feel *something*.' She bit her lip and cast her shameful eyes on the ground, where she then retrieved the book that fell out of my satchel earlier and placed it on her lap, underneath the tissue. 'Even though I know I shouldn't. And I suppose that's all, Father. I'm ready for my penance.' Once more, Anna dabbed the corner of her eye and blew her nose.

Her confession hit me like a ton of bricks. I didn't know where to begin. She was right by the laws of the Orthodox Church to exclude anybody else's sins from her own personal confession, but I had a feeling she wasn't the only one to blame, if she could be blamed at all.

'Did this occur one time? Multiple times?'

'Which one, Father? I've concealed truth once but felt useless multiple times.'

'Unchaste in deed?'

'Oh, he only did it once, I – ' she gasped, realizing her error and scurrying to cover it up, 'I mean – *it*. It only happened once.' Her head bowed in humiliation.

I bit my own lip and nodded, turning back to the readings and finishing my part. Then: 'Would you mind kneeling for me, Anna? I'll be just a moment while I grab my stole for this next part.' I reached for the hanger on the hook and unzipped the bag to retrieve my stole. I kissed it, said a silent prayer over it, placed it around my neck and lay the fringed end over her bowed head. I began reciting lines from the book. The confession weighed on me: victims of such heinous crimes should never feel like their burden needs to be confessed. But that was my opinion as a man not in collar. When I was; I had to respect their need to be cleansed and nourished through whatever spiritual means necessary. '...*that the Merciful God forgive you all things, through me a sinner, both in this world and in the world to come*...' I made the sign of the cross on the stole which still lay draped over her head and tried to focus my attention on finishing the Rite. I was struggling. '...*Glory to the Father, and to the Son, and to the Holy Spirit, now and ever, and unto the ages of ages, amen*.'

I had her rise to her feet and do her cross. After reading a final passage, I sat. I closed the book; placed it back in my satchel, pulled off my stole and set it back on the hanger. All the while Anna stood, watching, waiting.

'My penance, Father?'

I gestured to the seat beside me. 'Have a seat, Anna.' When she placed herself next to me, I reached for her hand, which I squeezed, and took her in my arms. 'You pray just as you have been, alright? Practice your Russian so you don't lose it. Confess regularly. Have some faith in yourself,' I advised, covertly plucking the collar from my shirt and sticking it in my satchel. 'And when you get to wherever it is that you're going, promise me one thing.'

'What, Father?'

'File a police report.'

At the sound of those last words, her hot tears dripped onto my neck and she nodded.

Second Taste

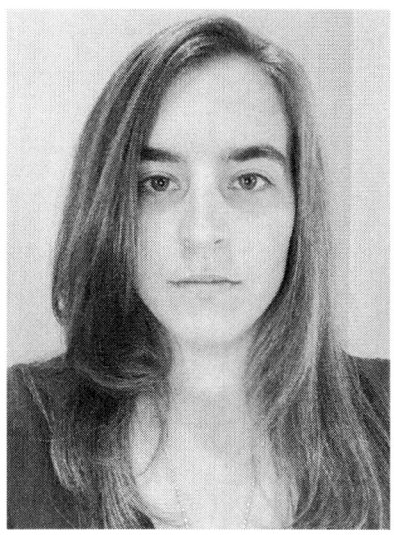

Alexandra is an elementary ESL teacher who splits her time between her hometown of Dallas, Texas and the Picardy region of northern France, where she currently teaches English in the public French schools. She holds a degree in education from Angelo State University and enjoys playing the violin, song-writing, reading, bowling, snowboarding, crossword puzzles, learning new languages, and genealogical research.

Finding the Music

by Cath Barton

I am an old woman and the restrictions of old age oblige me to take the elevator rather than the stairs now. But I cannot complain; the climate here in Southern California is benign and I am more than comfortably off. I have earned good money and still do, thanks to my music. My home is furnished with what my parents back in England would have called 'all mod cons'. It is what I said I wanted and I know that there are many who would envy me my lifestyle.

From my balcony I watch runners on the beach in the early morning. I admire the litheness of their limbs, their easy movement. Oh that they would turn, run up the stairs and bring the freshness of youth into my apartment. Such foolish thoughts! I have made my path in life and I cannot change it. But I cannot help thinking back, sometimes, to a colder shore on the other side of this continent, and to a time when, with my life in front of me, I had an encounter with an even more sprightly runner.

*

The sound was thin, a skein of elusive melody. Neither of the ladies showed any sign of having heard it. They were sitting on the running board of the car, collars up, gazing at nothing, because there was nothing to see on the beach. Just the flat expanse of yellow-grey sand and the thin line of small breaking waves where it met the blue-grey sea. The bulk of the Cadillac behind the ladies protected them from the wind, which had in it that day an edge of the viciousness of a winter only reluctantly giving way to spring.

I knew I should unpack the picnic basket and lay out the luncheon on the small table which I had erected in the lee of the car. It was, after all, my job. But I was curious about the mysterious sound and where it was coming from. As I hesitated, wondering whether I could stroll along the beach without incurring the displeasure of one or the other of my ladies, an elfin boy came into sight playing a flute. His bare feet made no mark upon the sand. As he skipped past I felt a pull to follow him, as if he were a modern-day pied piper, but like the ladies I was muffled in a winter coat and unable to move anywhere in a hurry in my heavy town shoes, unsuitable for the beach.

Soon the boy was a speck on the horizon, but his music seemed to linger on the wind for the whole of the noon hour, distracting me as I set out the sandwiches and poured glasses of lemonade for Miss Daisy and Miss Bertha, as they had insisted I call them from the beginning. I would have preferred the more formal use of their surname, but, as they said, there had to be a way of differentiating between them. And, said Miss Daisy, we were, after all, to be friends, were we not?

I had not taken this job to find friends. It was, for me, purely a way of earning money. I had no idea what I would do with the money, but I had been brought up to believe that with it I could buy anything I wanted. Probably even love, though that was far from my mind. I wanted freedom and I knew from watching other girls back home that love meant slavery. Those girls with the high cheekbones and translucent complexions that attracted the boys all looked, within a year of their marriage, drawn and tired. And if they were not already pushing a mewling infant in a pram they were full-bellied with the imminent prospect of that. But if I did not want to get married – and oh, believe me, I did not! – what was I to do? Work in a bank like other plain girls? Counting other people's money did not interest me. I wanted my own.

My aunt heard about the job, through a connection I never quite understood, but I knew she had been pally with an American GI during the war. People always said that word, 'pally', in a way which implied more, but I didn't care. Good luck to my Aunt Willis, as far as I was concerned, because it was thanks to her connections that I had fetched up on the Eastern seaboard as driver to the Misses Borne-Edgar. Not as strange a job for me as some of my mother's friends seemed to think. I'd driven ambulances during

Second Taste

the blitz in London. Tooling around New Hampshire in a shiny black Cadillac was a doddle after that.

At first it was exciting, driving the ladies here and there. When they went to luncheon at friends' houses I sat in the big downstairs kitchens and listened to all the gossip about who was doing what with (or to) whom in East Coast society. Each week I stashed another fat envelope of dollar bills into an Uncle Sam tin tea caddy which rapidly filled up, because whatever else they got up to and however parochial their interests, the people my ladies mixed with were generous tippers. And I, as a woman driver, was a novelty. It amused them to give me extra. Sometimes there were guys – I will not call them gentlemen – who wanted a little something in return and I could have taken offence, but I always gave them my sweetest smile, said politely that I was not at liberty to oblige them, and took their money. Why would I have qualms? They didn't. But I soon found that simply accumulating money was not enough. There was a need in me which it did not feed. A need I could not name.

It was Miss Daisy who had suggested the seaside picnic. It was, for her and her sister, something curiously daring, though for me merely another day's work. I expected nothing of it, and certainly not a passing sprite to dangle temptation unbidden in my path. But as I sat there with my elderly charges on the windy beach, thoughts came into my mind. An idea that coiled there, like a snake waiting to be charmed, ready to rise up when the right moment came.

That moment came sooner than I expected as next day neither of the ladies appeared at breakfast. Their maid pitter-pattered into the back kitchen, pink-cheeked with anxiety and said that the doctor must be called. They had both taken a chill at the beach, she said in a breathless whisper. To me this was ridiculous, we had all been so well wrapped up and none of us had so much as paddled in the sea. I told her not to worry, if they stayed in their beds and she kept them supplied with hot drinks they would soon be back to normal. I would, I said, go and fetch some proprietary remedies from the pharmacy in town.

Driving back in the car I took the longer route along the sea shore, and stopped off to take some breaths of the sea air atop the dunes. The wind was very strong now and there was no one below me on the beach, no sprite in sight. I drove back to the house. When I had delivered the medicines to the ladies' maid, I told the kitchen staff not to lay a place for me at luncheon; I had another errand to run.

It was on my own behalf that I set forth once more in the Cadillac. The boy behind the counter in the shop that I now entered had a scrubbed red forehead and eager eyes. He nodded at my request, scurried to the back of the store and brought back three long thin boxes. He left them with me, gesturing to me to take a look inside as he attended to a shrill-voiced woman behind me.

Inside each box was a silver-coloured flute. They seemed almost too shiny to touch with my working fingers and I had no idea how to choose between them. The shrill-voiced woman turned and saw the instruments on the counter. She pointed to one of them and told me it was the best make, I should definitely take it. I took it, handing over a wad of dollar bills. I turned to ask the woman if she knew of any teachers, but she was already out of the door. The boy said he had a phone number. He wrote it on the flute box, together with a name. It was not an inspiring name: Mr D Tooth. Not the sort of name the elfin player would have. But then I could hardly expect such a creature to be a teacher.

When I got back to the house the ladies were up and fretting for a ride out. I could not ring Mr Tooth until after supper and, that first time, there was no answer. Nor the following evening. I might have given up, but as I had no-one else to try I persisted and on the third attempt found him at home.

'I can't abide the name Tooth,' he confided at my first lesson. 'Makes people think of dental decay.' He shuddered. 'It's Mr T, okay?'

It was a relief when he asked me to call him that, far preferable to either the dry formality of his surname or the pseudo-familiarity

Second Taste

on which the Misses Borne-Edgar insisted. What his first name was I never discovered, but in my mind it was never anything as banal as David. Possibly Damian or Daniel. Or, more fantastically though certainly possible in America, Deangelo or Deon. But no matter, from that day on he was Mr T to me.

I could not conceal my new interest from anyone in the house, for I had to practice. Mr T advised half an hour a day. I followed his advice faithfully, for although he was a solid man, he was as alluring as the elfin character on the beach. But I soon came to realise that it was not so much Mr T as the music that fascinated me, nourished me and came to mean everything to me.

At first I wondered whether my practice would annoy the ladies, even though I always did it in my own time, and when Miss Bertha said she had a request I was fearful that it was that I should desist from my playing. To my amazement she asked if I would play at a small soiree they were holding, just a few friends for supper. Nothing too formal. An entertainment would please them.

Mr T clapped his hands with delight when I told him.

'There's nothing I like better than a challenge!' he said. 'And we will rise to it together.'

I asked Miss Bertha if my teacher might come along and play a duet with me. She asked his name. I told her that it was Mr Tooth and she giggled as she must have done as a schoolgirl, then drew herself up, gave a little nod of her head to the right as was her habit and said she would be very pleased if he would come.

In the little concert we presented classics from the French flute repertoire as well as some popular show tunes and Mr T slipped in a little virtuoso piece when – as I knew they would – the company cried for a solo from him. At the end of the evening I was flushed with pride, as indeed were my employers. From then on they would boast of being the only people in New Hampshire to have not only a female driver but also one who was 'such a fine' flute player. I spent some of my earnings on music, and then on a better flute for it was true, I did seem to have an aptitude.

One day, towards the end of September, I drove the Misses Borne-Edgar to the beach again. They sat on the running board of the Cadillac and I set out the sandwiches and lemonade. They gazed out on the expanse of sand and, beyond, small waves at the edge of the sea. The scene was much as it had been on that windy day of early spring when the elfin flautist had shown me the way. Except that there was a warmth in the air, a remnant of all the days of the summer.

'Do you remember the boy playing the flute we saw when we came here at the beginning of the season?' I asked the ladies. 'It was he who...'

'As I recall, my dear, we had the beach entirely to ourselves that day,' said Miss Daisy, interrupting me.

I looked to Miss Bertha, but she merely made a moue and shook her head. She was not one to argue with her sister.

We sat together quietly for a while, each of us thinking her own thoughts.

'It seems to me that there is music in the air now,' I essayed, at length.

'I hear only the wind,' said Miss Bertha, with an indulgent smile. 'But when we return to the house you must serenade us with your music.'

'Of course,' I said, with a smile, for I knew better than to pursue an argument with the ladies.

And later, as I played for them, I thought once more of the elfin boy, the one who had inspired me to take up the flute.

*

Second Taste

I was indeed a good flautist; it was not just my ladies who thought so. At the end of that summer I was due to return to England. But one of the people who had heard me play at the Misses Borne-Edgar's summer soiree got in touch with an invitation. It was a chance to play in an orchestra, to make a recording, he said. It would, he went on, be very much worth my while financially. I was flattered. I went to New York and became a session musician, playing in pick-up bands and trying everything on offer: the one-night stands, the drink, the drugs… I made money – plenty – but for all its glamour, the music business crushes you. By the time I turned thirty, I was numb, a victim like so many others of crazy hours, callous producers and – I won't deny it – my own weakness.

One night, walking on a beach alone at 2am, I fancied that I saw the elfin boy again, beckoning to me, reminding me about the music. The next day I checked into rehab. I got clean and I got respectable work. But I didn't trust folk after that. I've been alone for a long time. Of course my working days are over but sometimes I get out that first flute I bought in New Hampshire and I play some of the French music that Mr T taught me back when. I cry a little afterwards. And then I dry my eyes, go out onto my balcony and enjoy the caress of the warm breeze off the ocean.

Second Taste

Cath Barton is an English writer who lives in Wales. She won the New Welsh Writing AmeriCymru Prize for the Novella 2017 for *The Plankton Collector*, which will be published on 27 September 2018 by New Welsh Review under their Rarebyte imprint. She particularly likes to use visual images as prompts for her writing and is currently working on a collection of short stories inspired by the work of the sixteenth century Dutch artist Hieronymus Bosch, for which she has been awarded a place on the 2018 Literature Wales Mentoring Scheme.

Cath won 2nd place in the Dorset Fiction Award, October 2017. Recent publications: stories in *The Lonely Crowd, Fictive Dream, Spelk* and other flash fiction online. Forthcoming: stories in *Strix* and *Normal Deviation*.

She is a regular contributor to the online critical hub Wales Arts Review. More details about her writing at https://cathbarton.com/ Tweets @CathBarton1

Unsent

by Irma Goderdzishvili

1ˢᵗ May

I constantly wonder what you're thinking about. Whether you might be missing me or maybe you don't even think about me and it's just me who can't move on... I remember watching you, only three weeks ago, in the waves of the sea, topless, laughing, the sun on your beautiful face, your little round breasts just perfect... Much as I didn't want you to be without a top in front of lots of strangers, I said nothing. You were happy.

You found a heart-shaped stone and with your red nail varnish you wrote our names on it and the date. The stone is in our bedroom, but you aren't... Not an hour goes by when I don't have you on my mind. Life without you isn't life. It's become a form of torment.

11ᵗʰ June

You loved white blossom on strawberry plants, the smell of tomato leaves. Summer is back, but not you. I tell myself every day that you will be soon, regretting what you see was a dreadful mistake…

Time drags by and I cross off the weeks on the calendar. You got me that calendar, but you never said I'd be staring at it with such forlorn hope; that in fact I would hate it. These days and weeks waiting for a call or a text – I didn't know then that time would weigh so heavily...

And yet I worry – sometimes I notice that hours have passed without me thinking of you, and I dread a day may come when I don't think of you at all. Much as I don't like the way I feel right now, that would be even worse. When you love someone, it isn't just loving that person but loving yourself with that person, loving being loved and cared for.

Since you left, I've felt like half a man; no that's a lie – I feel like no one. All I know is that I long to see you again, hold you in my arms and touch your soft hair once more. And it may sound strange, but often all I want to do is just put my head in your lap and sleep. I haven't slept well since you left. I stare at the ceiling in the dark and put my head on your pillow and imagine you there next to me. Then I dream of our bodies together, how we won't be able to get enough of each other, how I'll want time to freeze so I can keep you with me, but even there in my dreams I'm scared that you'll leave me again. Even in my dreams I can't allow myself to believe that all will be well...

I go to work and come back to an empty home, I go to the gym and come back to an empty home, I go to a café or a pub and come back to an empty home. I put the lights on, the TV, the radio, I put the kettle on... I even look for holidays from time to time but it makes the loneliness worse...

1st September

It's after 3 a.m. now. I can't sleep. I always want to talk to you. Writing to you sometimes helps but I never have the courage to press the 'send' button. I fear you'll see how vulnerable I am, how badly I'm coping without you and then you'll never want to come back. I remember you telling me you hate weak men, the ones who cry over women, who can't stand on their own two feet, who depend on others to feel fulfilled and happy. I remember that and get scared to carry on writing, in case one day you come back and find all these letters...

I keep looking for reasons – what you really meant when you said this or that, why in the days before you left you slept with your back towards me, why you kept kissing me, caressing me on our last night together... And then you just walked out.

I think and think, but can't make sense of it. You showed so much love towards me, you looked so sad when you left. How could you do that? Why?

15th Dec

I've imagined you with someone else so many times and got myself upset. I just imagine you smiling to that someone, not even holding his hand or showing love in any way, and it breaks me. I want all your smiles for me. I need them like a medicine.

I went to see my parents last week. I never spoke about us, I still haven't told them you're gone. It's easier to live a lie. My mum asked how you were and I told her you were fine. She asked about our plans. She wants us to get married, she wants grandchildren. I said that I'd propose on your next birthday.

On my second day there, I suddenly felt that if I got in my car and drove for eight hours, you'd be in the house waiting for me. It was worth going up to Scotland just to feel that. I drove back that night, telling mum I had a call from work and had to be there next morning.

I loved feeling alive again and whole. I was thinking that if I drove very fast, if I got home before five in the morning, you'd be in our bed waiting for me. When I got in, I checked every room, knowing you couldn't be there, but wanting to prove to myself that miracles do happen. I just need to believe in them.

I was hoping you'd at least call that week or that month. I felt so close to you during my trip from my parents. But you never did.

Eight months now. If only I could forget you, if only I could stop missing you... I don't know where you live – if I did, I'd turn up on your doorstep and tell you all I've been writing, because I know you wouldn't shut the door on me... I'd say it to your face but I'm too scared to send you these emails...

27th Feb

I sometimes feel if I don't see you, I'll pass out. I was nourished when you were with me. Now it doesn't matter what I do, what I get or don't get for myself, I feel hungry and thirsty all the time. Remember that recipe for prawns? The dish we so enjoyed? It has no taste any more... I open a bottle of wine and have it whether I want it or not. I open your favourite box of chocolates and leave the ones you love in case you come soon. I look after your flowers in the conservatory, talk to them like you did, wanting you to see how I care for them. It's like I'm trying to prove to you that I'm all you could ask for. I want you to want me again.

3rd June

Your mum called today. I was having coffee when my phone rang and there was a picture of you and her on my screen. I looked and looked at it, not answering straight away. I hadn't heard your voice for a long time, I was scared and worried and nervous all at once. I cleared my throat and said 'hello', I think I said: 'hello, you', I'm not sure. I think I said something but maybe I didn't. My mouth was so dry, my lips were glued to each other.

She was calling to say you'd lost your battle with cancer. She said that before you left you'd been told you would lose both breasts and you didn't want me to see you that way. And yet, she said, you were hoping to hear from me every day – but when she wanted to call me you stopped her...

4th June

Why? How could you do that to me? To yourself? How could you doubt my love for you? Why couldn't I be with you? To help you through it, to be there right to the end, to do whatever I could. To hate the cancer inside you but embrace the person you are. How could you just leave me guessing for months? How could you make me think you didn't want me in your life any more, when you missed me too, when you wanted me too?

5th June

It was so much easier to live in hope, that one day you would come back! You'd only say a few words – that you wanted to be with me again, and then I'd wake up with you every morning and start my days feeling loved, fulfilled, content that when I returned home, it wouldn't be an empty house, but there would be *you*, some of your music playing, lights on, dinner in the oven, your little chocolates by the radio, a good film to watch and then I would cuddle up and go to sleep with you.

I had all these things, I waited for all these things, and now all I feel is anger and pain and disappointment. Did you think it would alter my feelings for you? Were you trying to protect me? Were you afraid I would see you as less than perfect? I feel so hurt – yet how can I feel anger towards the girl I love, who has left me now, left the world? I try to reach an acceptance – it was your choice, your life, you who had to fight the disease, so what right have I to question it? But just when I think I've got it, my mind spins off again in hopelessness and confusion.

8th June

I attended your funeral. I saw you. I saw you before the funeral too. Your mum had chosen a picture of you which I took while we were on holiday. She chose the flowers on your coffin, freesias – orange, white, yellow and purple. You so loved freesias. After you left, I kept on buying them to keep the house smelling as it did when you lived there.

Second Taste

The church hall smelt of freesias. The smell was so strong, I saw you getting out of your picture and walking towards me. I could see you so well… you were wearing the white linen dress you wore on our first date. Freesias were everywhere and I kept wondering what they would look like in your hands, in your hair, by your lovely ears which had small butterfly earrings...

Your mum talked about you lots, about your last weeks and days in hospital. Your sister cried; your nieces were there, looking so sad. The little one isn't little any more, she looked so grown up. I looked at them and wished you could stand between them, hold their hands. I wished your mum could see you standing there by the freesias, smiling…

9th June

From my room as I write, I can see a blackbird sitting on the fence. I see three rose buds which will open any time this week in the corner of the garden. I hear the cars from the road, not many but one or two from time to time.

The funeral helped. A little. Perhaps with every passing day, it'll be easier. It's well-known, isn't it? The healing passage of time. That's what everyone says. But I can't see that right now. Because right now, I would do anything to be able to put my head on your chest and hear your heartbeat, so perfectly clear through the scars…

Second Taste

I was born in the Republic of Georgia. I graduated from Georgia University where I studied English. I went to the UK at the age of 20 to continue my studies and that's where I live now with my husband and two children.

Mother Nurture

by Laura Geall

I sit in the surprisingly colourful waiting room, as I do every Tuesday and Friday morning. I always choose the same chair in the corner, it's the comfiest one in the room because it has one cushion more than the others. I don't normally use the surplus comfort for its actual purpose. Instead, I sit the cushion on my lap, like a pet, so that I can cover my legs and play with the tassels that cover each side to give my fingers something to do. To stop them scratching at my skin and feeling the bones underneath.

The other reason that I love this chair is because it's in the corner, so it means I have a view of the whole room and can people-watch to my heart's content, but I remain pretty much invisible to everyone except the receptionist. She looks at me and I smile at her. She's got such a sweet face, with soft, round cheeks that make it look as if her mouth is stuffed with cotton balls or marshmallows. What I'd give to have a face like hers.

I remove the cushion from my lap and walk over to her, unsteady on my legs after sitting for so long.

'Hi Trish.'

'Hello, lovely.'

'I need to use the restroom, but I know my appointment time was…' I look at the white clock on the wall above her head, 'five minutes ago.'

She smiles at me in apology.

'Am I ok to go?'

'Yes, you are. I'm sorry, lovely, he's running really late today.' She looks at me as if it's the worst thing in the world.

I laugh to try to put her at ease. 'It's ok, Trish, I think I'd actually be surprised if he was on time.'

I turn and head towards the bathroom. I feel the pity burning into my back as I walk. Not just from Trish, but everyone else waiting. I don't like moving from my hiding spot in the corner, being out in the open for everyone to stare at.

I didn't need to go, but I needed to get up. When I walk, I feel like my legs are giant needles, sending a sharp pain through my body as the pin end hits the floor, but I have to make myself do it. If I sit down for too long, I may never get up.

I lean over the sink, looking down. One of my hands grips the marble and I use the other to splash cold water over my face. I keep my eyes closed as I reach for the tissue that I know is immediately on my right. I dry my face and when I remove the tissue I forget, for a moment, to keep my eyes closed and I see myself in the mirror.

I have avoided mirrors for the last week. Purposefully.

I've gotten worse.

My cheeks are so thin it looks as if someone has covered the insides with glue and stuck them to my gums. The skin underneath my eyes looks as if it's made of quicksand, rapidly sinking and making my eyes bulge like a cartoon villain.

As I stare at myself intently, I see small, moving black dots behind my eyes and I can feel my legs starting to go underneath me. I grip the sink with both hands and lower myself onto my knees, breathing deeply. I concentrate on the sound of the automatic air freshener in the corner as it whirs, ready to release its next puff. If I sit down, take deep breaths and think of something else, I might not faint.

I don't know how long passes, but I try and make myself feel better as quickly as I can. I reluctantly stand up. If I'm in here too long, Trish will get worried and come looking for me. Leaving her post to find a lost soldier.

Second Taste

Just before I leave, I see my thin face again. I look into my sunken eyes and tell myself that it's not my fault. When people see me, I either get looks of pity, or of judgement. Most people assume I have an eating disorder. But this is not something that I've done to myself. I have a rare condition that means I can't digest food properly. My body tries, and it causes itself so much pain in doing so, that in the end, it rejects it. As a result of my body not getting the nourishment it needs, it's weak and thin, like the ice covering a pond in winter as it starts to melt. The kids daren't skate on it in case it cracks completely.

I look at myself one final time and go back into the waiting room. I teeter along the corridor, not only because of my weak legs, but also because I want to draw as little attention to myself as possible.

Trish catches me before I walk over to my corner seat again. 'He's ready for you now. You can go right on through.'

'Thanks.' I continue walking to the door that's so familiar to me.

I walk inside and Doctor Green turns, blinking in shock as he sees me. I must be bad. In the time he's been treating me, he's never reacted to how I look.

I sit on the edge of the bed, in my usual place.

'How's your daughter?' I ask, as always, while he pokes and prods me.

He diagnosed me the same week he had his baby daughter. She's four years old now. You'd think I'd be jealous of hearing about her health, but I love thinking about his little girl, who'd been given life in the same week mine was taken away.

They'd just been away on holiday, so I hadn't seen him for a couple of weeks.

'It's strange not seeing you here with your mum,' he says.

Second Taste

I look down. My mum used to come to every appointment with me. 'I know. I think it was getting too hard for her.'

'I guess you're eighteen now, so it's up to you. I went away just before your birthday, how was it?'

I smile, thinking back to the birthday card he gave me just before he went. He had signed it from 'Doctor Green' and the little scribble next to it was his daughter's handwriting. 'I went out clubbing and got smashed.'

We both laughed. He knows I didn't, couldn't, even. But he doesn't press me. I don't want to tell him that I spent my birthday evening throwing up the meal my mum had made me, as she sat on the floor of the bathroom next to me, holding my hand.

'I wish your mum was here.'

I look up at him. 'It's bad, isn't it?'

He sits down next to me and takes his hand in mine. I look down and compare our skin. Tan against translucence.

'You've gotten a lot worse since I last saw you,' he says, looking down at our hands too. 'I think you need to come and spend some time in hospital. We can look after you there. We can get you on a drip and try and get some calories in you. Your body is failing, Hannah. I'm sorry, I think this is the only way now.'

We both let it be silent for a while. I think back to the last time I was in hospital, when I was fed through a tube and I had to lie in bed all day. They put me in a bed next to a window to try and console me, but it felt like a cruel placement. I had lain there, looking at the world turning outside, whilst the only movement in the brightly lit hospital room was the sound of the heart monitors, beeping out of sync with each other.

'Ok.'

He smiles. 'Brilliant, Hannah. Pack a bag when you get home and tell your mum. When you come in for your next appointment, bring her with you and we'll get you set up.'

I get off the bed, slowly and steadily. 'Thanks, Dr Green.'

'No problem. I'll see you very soon.'

I head towards the door but turn just as I touch the handle. 'Thank you, Dr Green, for everything.'

'It's no problem.' His eyes flicker with concern. 'It will be ok Hannah, I promise you that.'

'I know.'

I smile at him and he smiles back.

I turn the cool handle and head out the door.

'Bye, Trish, see you soon.'

'Bye, lovely.'

I go through the automatic doors and into the sunshine. My taxi is waiting there, to take me home.

When I get in, my mum is sitting at the kitchen table, biting her nails.

'There you are, sweetie, I was so worried about you.'

'I'm ok, Mumma.'

She looks up at me and her cheeks are glistening.

'Come on, I'm tired. Let's sit on the sofa for a while.'

'Ok. How did it go? What did Dr Green say?'

'We'll talk about it later. I'm tired now, Mumma.'

The sun is coming in through the window, covering the sofa with light. Mum opens the window to let the fresh air in.

'Is that ok?' She looks at me, she knows how I shiver all the time, with barely enough skin to keep me warm.

'It's perfect.'

She sits on the sofa, her back against the armrest and I lie between her legs, my head resting on her chest, like I've done since I was a kid. I can hear her heart beat. I place my hand on my own chest. Her heart is beating so much quicker than mine.

I look down at my legs. As I curl them up, my kneecaps become even more prominent, stretching my skin so it looks as if it will snap.

I close my eyes and nestle into my Mumma and finally, I feel warm.

She kisses the top of my head and hugs me so tight that I fear I might break in two. Her heartbeat grows faster still and her skin is so close to mine that it feels like it's passing through, transferring some of her life into me.

I open my eyes and, though it's probably just the bright sunlight playing tricks on me, I look down and I no longer see pale skin with bruised bones jutting out underneath. I compare my arm to my mum's and they're the same colour. I put my hand up to my cheek and they feel plump, like Trish's.

I close my eyes again, with my hand on my heart, listening to the beat slowly fading. I don't need nurses and drips and fake nourishment through IVs. I need my home and I need this love from my Mumma.

Second Taste

Laura Geall was born in Curacao, an island in the Caribbean, and moved back to England with her family when she was five. She graduated with an English degree from Bournemouth University, where she received a First Class grading for her creative dissertation. She loves to read, write and travel. She particularly enjoys road trips across the USA. She has now qualified to teach English as a Foreign Language and has tutored in Budapest, Prague and Malta so far. She lives in Lewes, East Sussex with her dog, Max.

Laura's piece of flash fiction titled *Let's Fly Away* was published in *The Great British Write Off – Timeless Echoes* in 2016, an anthology printed by Forward Poetry. This was part of a competition, where she was shortlisted to the Top 20 out of over a thousand entries. She has also won The Writer's Notebook June competition with her short story *Alone*, which was chosen by the Editor and won because it had the most votes on social media.

Twitter handle: @Laura_Geall

Second Taste

And Came the Flying Pig

by Anais Jay

She lay on the reclined car seat beside mine, her legs folded up to her chest and her socked feet crossed at the ankles. The orange glow of sunrise touched her freckled face. Even asleep, I thought, Natasha looked brave.

With my free hand, I pulled the discarded blanket up to her shoulder, and with the other I steered the car a little to the right to let the van behind us overtake in the narrow road.

The van honked its thanks, and Natasha jolted upright. She searched her bag and brought out a stuffed toy and some thread. The toy wasn't finished: the back was still to be stitched up. Her fingers fumbled with the thread to loosen the tangles. I switched on the dome light for her.

She blinked up at it, then at me. 'Oh right, you're here. Morning.'

I smiled at the road ahead. We'd been driving through barely lit roads since midnight to get to Ilocos before noon – hadn't she even noticed I was there?

I comforted myself with the fact that she'd insisted on going alone; it was her father, Sir Edgar, who'd called me to ask if I'd accompany her. At first I supposed it was because he knew I had the time – I'd recently quit my job and split with my girlfriend. But subsequent messages made me realise that although he hadn't seen me for years, he still trusted me to keep his daughter safe.

I glanced at her from the corner of my eye. Sir Edgar still viewed her as a little girl, which made it harder for me to see the twenty-three year old woman she was now. Perhaps it had something to do with it being my birthday. Thirty. The first dawning horror of getting old.

'What's that toy you're busy with?' I asked.

'A pig.' She turned it towards me. The round, black beads for eyes seemed to stare at me, waiting for my praise. 'The Flying Pig. I haven't attached the wings yet.'

'No kidding! I haven't seen that since….since you were twelve!' I took the pig from her and sat it atop the steering wheel. 'The cloth is a bit paler than I remember. But other than that it's identical.'

'You can say it,' she said, after a while. 'You haven't seen it since the Flying Pig became our company's last hurrah. And here we are many years later, still broke. I mean, I am. You're definitely not.'

The line of trees by the roadside limited our view of the sky, making it look like a river overhead. The sky in Makati City never looked this clear.

'Actually, I remember it best as the first toy you designed. All because the doctor forbade Ma'am Ruth from eating pork. Compensation for having to give up bacon.' When she didn't respond to that, I asked if she was giving it as a get well present for Lukas.

She snatched the toy and resumed stitching the pig's back. 'I promised him I'd make him one but I never got around to doing it until now.'

'You never did mention what Luke is sick with. Nor why he's in Ilocos instead of Makati or Taguig. Some of the best hospitals in the country are there. I'm sure his family can afford it with all the restaurants they run down south.'

'The recipient's a relative of one of the surgeons there.'

'I'm sorry? I don't follow.'

Nash pushed the needle into multiple folds of fabric and pulled at the thread. 'Luke donated his kidney to a sixty-five year old stranger.'

I parked the car on the side of the road. Nash looked around us and, seeing nothing amiss, stared at me in confusion. 'I can sew while the car's moving.'

I gazed at her, dumbfounded. 'But... Why would he do that?'

She shrugged, feigning indifference, but her face had turned red. 'Don't know. What's done is done.'

We made our first stopover in Vigan. The white van from earlier parked in front of my car, and a group of couples scurried out to take pictures of the Spanish colonial houses.

Nash walked past them and into the nearest restaurant. All my attempts to start a conversation were met with silence. She spent the next hour seated on the Narra chair across from mine, staring at the fried eggs, burnt *tapa* and lopsided tower of rice, while absently fiddling with the Flying Pig on her lap.

I asked her if she was all right. She said, 'Absolutely,' but wouldn't look me in the eye.

When we reached Ilocos Norte, her composure cracked. She kept cursing the thread and telling me not to hurry because she still needed to attach one of the wings. I slowed down and took the long way to the city proper, but we still made it to the hospital car park in twenty minutes.

I cut the engine. 'We're here.'

Nash peered outside the window. She checked her watch. 'We're early. It's only ten. It's too early.'

'I thought you wanted to spend more time with Lukas?'

She opened and closed her mouth in a couple of false starts. She gestured to the toy on her lap. 'The pig can't fly with only one wing! I'm not done yet. It can't be the Flying Pig like this! Better no wing at all than just one, it's a mess, look, all lop-sided...'

I held my hand up to cut her short, but she kept up a frantic jabbering till I'd driven us out of the car park. The local people glanced our way, aware of cars that weren't one of theirs. I spoke to a street vendor to ask where the windmills were, and a couple of elderly passers-by huddled outside our car to give us varying directions.

The women peered in to see Nash, whom they presumed was my girlfriend. What a lucky guy, they said. What's that she's making?

We drove to the windmills in silence. Nash propped her bare feet upon the dashboard to hold the toy in place on her knees. Inside my pocket, my phone kept vibrating. Missed calls. Text messages. Birthday greetings no doubt. Followed by questions about my plans for the future.

I parked the car beside the square boulders that served as barrier. Past it, a sandy hill led down to the beach where giant white windmills turned with the prompting of the sea breeze.

I got out of the car and stood on top of a boulder and spread my arms to the wind. 'Brilliant!' I shouted, pointing at the sea, but Nash was bent over her work, frowning furiously. I shrugged and turned round again, wondering what it would be like to be a windmill.

Then the car door slammed behind me and Nash was tugging at my shirt, the pig in her hand. 'Do you know how to stitch on the wings so the threads aren't visible? I've been redoing it a hundred times and I can't get it right.'

I studied her needlework to see where she'd gone wrong. 'Maybe.' I'd spent enough time watching her mother make toys to get a good idea of how it was done. 'I'll give it a go anyway.'

She climbed the boulder and crouched next to me. 'Hey, sorry for my temper.'

'You were much worse when you were eight and I had to babysit you.'

'Fun times, huh?'

'We're remembering it differently,' I said, smiling. 'But I do miss those times. I miss your big house and the games we played with your brother. All the laughing and crying over silly things.'

'Ben was always happy to have you around.' She cupped her face with both hands and pouted. 'I pretended not to enjoy your company, but you won me over with the pranks you pulled on our maids.'

'I'm sorry, Nash.'

'What for all of a sudden?' she asked.

I lowered the toy to me knee. 'Your family treated me well even though I was just your driver's son. When Sir Edgar sent me to school, I promised myself I'd repay him by being there for each one of you no matter what it costs me. I'd give you a kidney if you need it, but I'm not sure under what circumstances I'd do it for a stranger. I'm sorry I can't say anything helpful about this matter with Lukas.'

She embraced herself to keep warm. The wind swept her red-dyed hair away from her face. 'I don't think words achieve much. Nothing I said changed his mind.'

'What's his reason?'

'He thinks he's done nothing worthwhile in his life.' She dabbed the cuffs of her denim jacket over her eyes. 'That moron. That idiot. It's almost like an excuse to die, but I couldn't tell that to his face. He looked like a different man after he made the decision to donate.'

'He didn't give you anything particular? Something more...valid?'

'His explanation actually made it worse,' she said. 'I was in a minor car accident five months ago and I ended up needing stitches on my head. He told me it scared him. When he saw the stitches and the blood on my clothes, he put himself in my shoes and thought if he was the one in the accident and died right there and then, his life would've been for nothing. The worst part is he expects me to understand that because I was the one in the accident, but I don't. I tried but his logic ends up sounding more stupid to me the more I think about it. All I can think of is that he's willingly putting his life on the line for a stranger. A guy that's already been lucky to get as far as he has.'

'When was the operation?'

'Two days ago. The nurse informed me. He's okay. So is the old man. Now I just look like the bad guy for trying to stop him.'

'His family?'

'Infuriated. But I think they're coming over tomorrow to check on him.'

'Nash?'

'Yes?'

'You're not a bad person,' I said. I put my hand on her head. 'It's okay to be angry and confused and sad and relieved all at the same time. Wanting to keep him safe and healthy doesn't make you a bad person.'

Nash mopped her face with the sleeve of her jacket. 'I'd have given my heart to mama if that could've saved her, or at least granted her one day to eat all the bacon she wanted,' she said. 'I'd donate mine to you if you need it. But not to a stranger.'

'Don't worry, I'll try not to need it.'

Second Taste

Nash scowled at me, and she then broke into laughter.

I went with her to the hospital only as far as the lobby. She took one step forward, stopped, and then reached back to squeeze my hand. In those seconds of contact, I felt like the adult I should be, strong and dependable enough for others to lean on. But as her grip loosened and she went on her way, I realized that while I feared losing people I loved, I also feared the idea of losing myself. The passage of time. The struggle for a worthwhile existence. Things I still had to come to terms with.

Returning to the car, I found the Flying Pig on the driver's seat. I reached for it with the intention of bringing it over to Lukas's recovery room, but stopped to stare at the now finished product.

Nash designed this character that supposedly grew wings so it could escape angry chefs and live in liberty somewhere no one wanted it fried. When I questioned the purpose of the pig now that it wouldn't be turned into bacon, she answered me with one word – hope.

'Just because it stops to be one thing doesn't mean it stops to exist altogether,' she said. 'It will give mama hope that this thing she loves eating, she can also love as a toy that makes her hopeful when her illness gets too much.'

I wondered if the toy was really meant for Lukas, or if she tried to recreate it to give herself tangible hope to cling to.

Using the extra cloth in her bag, I stitched a cape onto the pig, and I imagined it greeting me: 'Happy birthday!' And saying that if a pig could fly, then I could also be something unexpected.

Anais Jay dreamt of being a doctor, a senator, and even a soldier, but ended up instead as the co-owner of a Philippine-based education consultancy and a writer of stories that border on strange. Her social anxiety scurries away when she finds people who love books as much as she does, which she believes is proof that prose heals. If she's not working on her manuscript or slaving away at work, you'll find her cooped up in a cozy place eating Cheetos while marveling at Haruki Murakami's novels.

www.anaisjaywrites.wordpress.com

The Climber

by John Paul Davies

'What's he doing on top of a church, exactly?' D.I. Proudwell asked.

'A one-man conga? How should I know?' said Sergeant Tollemache.

Most of Proudwell's enquiries were met in this way – amusing if the ludicrous case had fallen into anyone else's lap.

'Can't the PCs bring him down?'

'He's been asking for you, Ray,' said Tollemache. 'Says he won't budge unless you're there. Quite touching, really.'

The bane of Proudwell's professional life, John Dougall had several strings to his bow: local drunk, public urinater and unofficial Town Crier, filling St. James' Square each day with his unintelligible warbling.

Serial climber could now be added to that dubious résumé. Proudwell figured that this, Dougall's third climb in as many weeks, placed him firmly into the serial category.

Dougall's aerial debut had consisted of climbing a floodlight at Archer's Park. His attempt at providing the half-time entertainment backfiring, the football match was abandoned shortly afterwards. Not even the death-defying leap from the top of the floodlight to the roof of the main stand had redeemed Dougall in the supporters' affections.

Next came the conquest of Lidl for this urban Edmund Hillary. The former star of TV's 'Bargain Hunt', David Dickinson, had officially opened a new store on Main Street, the ribbon cutting facing little competition on a Saturday morning in the village.

Second Taste

Watching from the roof of the premium-priced emporium, can of Special Brew in hand, was John Dougall – savouring the moment after his vertical exertion. Below, it was difficult to tell who'd been the most embarrassed – the local dignitaries or the mahogany-tanned antique-dealer.

'And what am I expected to do when I get there?' asked Proudwell.

'Race him to the top?' Tollemache's response was greeted by general uproar in the open-plan office. Proudwell suspected that he would not hear the end of this assignment. He resigned himself to traipsing over to St. Catherine's Church, feigning interest as the fire brigade brought Dougall down. A night in the cells, then Dougall, or 'The Doog' as he was commonly known, would be released to climb again.

How exactly had he scaled a church anyway? Even Hillary would have at least planned the expedition for weeks beforehand. Such challenges seemed to require no second thought to the perpetually pissed.

'Don't forget your climbing boots, Ray!'

The fire engine was waiting when Proudwell pulled up at St. Catherine's. PC Aldridge stood beside it, smirking as his superior approached. Tollemache had evidently kept him up to speed with events at the station.

One of the firemen shouted down to Proudwell: 'There's no bloody way I'm goin' up! We're on strike next week – I'm not breakin' me neck for that nutcase!'

Proudwell scoured the churchtop for Dougall, finding no sign of the illicit climber among the gargoyles.

Second Taste

He grabbed the loudhailer from Aldridge. 'Dougall!' he barked, aiming the hailer's funnel skyward. 'Are you coming down from there anytime today?'

Proudwell saw his request declined non-verbally: a flicked V-sign held momentarily over the edge of the parapet, then withdrawn. The firemen watched from the engine's cabin with their feet up, enjoying the free entertainment on show.

Hearing a car door slam behind him, Proudwell turned to see Reverend Jameson approaching, ready for that evening's Service of Reconciliation.

Proudwell tried the alcoholic ascender again: 'Dougall! This is your last chance! We'll send the crane up!'

'Is there any way up through the church?' Proudwell asked Aldridge. 'The belfry?'

'Nah, been blocked up for years,' the PC replied. 'We had a look earlier.'

Reverend Jameson strode towards Proudwell, quickly using all of his ecumenical wisdom to gauge the situation. 'John Dougall up there, is he?'

He turned his attention to the roof before anyone could answer. 'Drunkard! Come down from there this second!' He appealed to Proudwell, 'Can't you do *anything*? People will be arriving soon for the evening service. We can hardly conduct matters with this stooge racing across the roof!'

'Sorry, Reverend, we'll have the bast– I mean, *fellow*, down as soon as possible.'

Proudwell, becoming increasingly desperate, attempted to persuade Aldridge and the firemen again: 'Come on, one of you lads will have to go up. Talk him down.'

'Tried that before you came, sir,' said Aldridge. 'The Doog said he'd only answer to Ray Proudwell. Oh, and the inflatable landing mat's on its way.'

'Well you have been bloody busy, then,' said Proudwell. 'Must admit, had you down as a complete waster before.'

'I don't care which one of you goes up! I want Dougall down this instant!' The Reverend was red-faced and spluttering now. 'No respect for anything, these people. No wonder this country's gone to the dogs!'

A group of local kids had pulled up on their bikes, grinning at the flustered detective, the reddening Reverend.

'Why can't you leave him alone? He's happy up there, that dosser!'

'Yeah, what harm's he doing anyway? Lousy gets!'

D.I. Proudwell found himself alone in the fire engine crane, rising slowly alongside the chapel wall. A small crowd had formed below, monitoring his progress: the firemen working the crane, the children watching open-mouthed, the Reverend stern and silent. Others arrived – perhaps the Reverend's flock ready for the evening service – and soon followed the upward gaze of the crowd, tracking Proudwell's ascent.

From his lofty position, the mechanical whirr of the rising crane drowned out any sound below. Approaching the stone parapet, he wondered how long Dougall would drag the sorry affair out for. Perhaps that draining day on the stadium roof would seem mere moments compared to what lay ahead.

The crane neared the parapet, the sky slowly bruising like a boxer's face under prolonged punishment. Knuckles whitening, Proudwell gripped the crane's sides, held his breath and waited.

Second Taste

The ringing in his ears started, his stomach turning as adrenalin flooded his veins – the vertiginous symptoms he was becoming familiar with, thanks to Dougall. A lemming-type syndrome gripped him, trilling his nerves, insisting he should throw himself off the crane. Proudwell tried not to look down again.

The climber eventually came into view, sitting with his back against the stone wall, staring straight ahead. Dougall's face was set and solemn, his features obscured by shadow.

Without looking over the edge, Proudwell held a thumb out to the firemen below, and the crane shuddered to a stop. Dougall showed no reaction to the detective's presence, perhaps contemplating where to go from here, which public monument to tackle next.

'Coming down now, Dougall?'

The Doog turned his head to look at Proudwell, as though only just noticing the other man.

'You mean you've come all this way – cheated, like – and you're not even gonna get onto the roof? What kinda story's that to tell your kids? 'Well I got up there and old matey came straight down with me'. Pathetic! Where's your sense of adventure, man?'

Proudwell hesitated. He had expected to find a slumped drunk, a nutter who could be lured down with a whiskey bottle, not this lucid character.

Below, the crowd continued to swell, their speculating voices seeming impossibly distant, merging into one deep murmur.

'Just get on the crane, John. You're not in any trouble, you know. We can sort this out on the ground.'

'Don't you feel like him, sometimes?' Dougall gestured towards something just out of Proudwell's eyeline. The detective felt his stomach lurch as he contemplated stepping onto the roof, his grip

Second Taste

on the crane's ledge tightening. The crowd's anticipation was tangible, watching the clouds speed past Proudwell's head.

Proudwell summoned the courage to look across the precipice, seeing the frog-faced gargoyle Dougall must have meant. Fondling its petrified part, the grotesque figure grinned lewdly at the crowd below.

'To ward off evil, they were for. You know, when they were building this place.'

'Come on, John, let's just get down from here, eh?' said Proudwell, attempting to steady his wavering voice. 'We'll say no more about this.'

'Buildings like these – look at the work that's gone into them. All those stones laid by hand.'

On the cusp of a panic attack, Proudwell forced his feet to move towards the edge of the crane. He realised he would have to jump the miniscule gap to the church roof – a space that in his agitated state had expanded to the width of a canyon.

'No one's been up here for donkey's years, do you know that? Buildings like these…who cares what goes on inside them, eh? No one *sees* things, these days. No one looks up anymore. Not that lot down there, hunched over their screens. Like cyborgs with those white plugs in their ears.'

The crowd saw Proudwell complete the short leap between crane and roof, and cheered.

'Sit down, chief,' The Doog said.

The detective breathed deeply, his heart hammering.

'You're alright now.' Dougall's voice became strangely melodic. 'It's only man-made stress, what you've got.'

Second Taste

In the quiet afforded by the battlements, the dark-slated spires, the losing light, Proudwell felt some of his anxiety begin to subside. He was no longer aware of the crowd below.

The crane remained like an outstretched arm, silent steel against ancient stone.

Proudwell sat down next to Dougall. Both men studied the gargoyles, the distant hills nestled on the horizon.

The clouds surrounded them, darkening steadily.

Enlightenment

by Kriss Nichol

She saw the retreat advertised in the *Lonely Planet Guide* and was intrigued. After six months being the only woman in the Field Office, she needed some nourishment for the soul.

The following morning Sarah asked her work colleagues if anyone had heard of it. There was an exchange of 'looks' between them, followed by vigorous head shaking.

'I thought I'd go this weekend but I've no idea where it is.'

More exchanges of 'looks', this time accompanied by rapid Nepali, too quick for her to understand.

'What?' she asked.

Eventually it was Santosh, the teaboy, who answered. 'Is in hills, Madam. Many bad men in hills.'

'Really? Is there a problem?'

He shrugged and gave a sideways head wobble. 'No, Madam.'

Sheepish looks from the rest were followed by an assertion, 'No, Madam. No problem.'

The men chattered and gesticulated amongst themselves, hands flying, then Santosh said, rather reluctantly, 'I take you.'

'You don't have to do that. Just tell me how to get there.'

He looked to the others who suddenly started examining their paperwork. He returned his gaze to her and sighed. 'Sorry, Madam. Not possible. I must take.'

The others enthusiastically agreed. There was nothing left to say.

Second Taste

They met on Saturday in Thamel at 6 a.m. It was a sweet-sky kind of day. One that makes your heart sing with possibilities. Santosh bounced up on his battered sit-up-and-beg Indian bike and Sarah perched on a gleaming second-hand competition mountain bike purchased from a Peace Corps volunteer returning to the US.

Eventually they left the city behind and started the long cycle uphill where Sarah puffed and wheezed, glad of the breeze and the sixteen gears on her bike. Santosh, with no gears, pedalled as though he were on the flat, his skinny frame only slightly bent forward as his legs pumped up and down. Below them, Kathmandu was visible through a pall of pollution that reminded Sarah of the mists and sea-fog of home. Ahead the road curved as it spiralled up the mountain. To either side were dried out shrubs, stones, marigolds and lizards. Above, the sun bore down relentlessly. Sarah regretted not wearing a hat.

Just before midday, when the heat was unbearable, the retreat became visible. It was an adobe-style build of mud over sticks with an archway entrance, low walls of mud bricks surrounding a complex of huts, and in the centre was a large circular building and nearby a fountain jetted upwards from a pool of shimmering water. Bountiful gardens offered shade and delicious scents of blossom wafted on the breeze.

Despite the numerous rests, Sarah was nauseous and dizzy. Clambering off the bike, her bum and stomach muscles shrieked in agony. They parked at the entrance, against the archway, and Sarah hobbled to the metal gate, desperate to get out of the sun. Attached to a wooden notice board at the side of the gate, posters in various languages stated a programme of weekend retreats. The following weekend was a Hindu holiday so Sarah would be off work from Thursday till Monday. She pointed this out to Santosh but he only frowned and nodded. She noticed another poster, handwritten this time, above the programme of dates, stating: 'Visitors attending retreats must participate in ALL activities'.

'That's a bit odd – I wonder why they're compulsory?'

Santosh shrugged.

There was no bell, so Sarah opened the gate and waddled through. Santosh, looking decidedly uncomfortable, followed. Sarah's legs were wobbly with exhaustion so she found a seat in the shade, just inside the entrance. Plonking down, closing her eyes, she surrendered for a while. Birds chattered, cawed, chukked and warbled around her in wave after wave of sound. Interspersed were the buzz of insects and bees, the whisper of leaves in the breeze and the swish of grass from small animals or lizards behind her. She was aware of her hair stuck to her forehead, sweat cooling on her face and the knots in her stomach loosening. She relaxed, drifting into a state of semi-consciousness, until she was disturbed by Santosh addressing her.

'Madam!'

Struggling to focus, she watched him nod in the direction of the garden. As her eyes adjusted to the glare she saw a vision in maroon robes walking towards them. The man was young, probably around thirty, and his thick, brown-black hair cascaded to his waist. But it was his face, perfectly proportioned and extremely beautiful, that made Sarah suddenly forget her pains. He approached, bowing in *Namaste*, and asked permission to join her. Whilst he did not address Santosh directly, he appraised him with barely hidden curiosity. She introduced Santosh as a friend, to which Santosh smiled; the monk raised an eyebrow.

After a little chit-chat Sarah disclosed the reason for her visit was to check out the retreat with a view to returning the following weekend. She gazed into clear dark-brown eyes, aware of plump ruby-red lips moving in speech.

'Would you like a tour of the centre?'

She nodded like someone demented. Santosh looked less keen.

Second Taste

As they walked, she tried hard to pay attention to his words, unsettled by the closeness of his body, the sensuousness of his movements. He took them past abundant flower beds where jasmine, frangipani, mimosa and datura harmonised with cacti. Past mango, lemon, fig and banana trees straining with fruit to the central area where the circular building stood. As they drew near, a few male heads popped up and watched them.

'This is the meditation centre,' the monk said, indicating with a graceful upward movement of his right arm.

Sarah looked back at the men watching them and reasoned they must be beginners to be so easily distracted from their meditations.

Inside, the building was panelled in wood, the floor decorated with sumptuous rugs and embroidered cushions, the windows held no glass.

Their tour ended beside the fountain and pool that was filled with huge golden carp. Placed on top of a low wall surrounding the pool were cushions for seating, reminiscent of some of the expensive hotels in Kathmandu. As they made to sit down the monk placed himself between Sarah and Santosh, turning his body towards her so that she had his full attention. Sarah felt flattered, till she looked at poor Santosh who was excluded by this move. She smiled encouragement at him. His smile back was thin.

'I understand the retreat next weekend is to connect the spiritual with the physical. Can you tell me more about it please? There doesn't seem to be anything on the board to say whether there are lectures, guided mediations or periods of silence.'

The monk smiled. 'The problem with the West is that it separates body from spirit. Enlightenment is when a person finds the truth about life and stops being reborn. Buddhists believe a person can become enlightened by following the Middle Way, a way of life that is neither a life of ease and enjoyment nor a harsh life, living on the minimum of the most basic necessities. We, here, believe in uniting the body with the spirit from where one is better equipped to start on the Path. '

Sarah smiled back. She tried again. 'Will there be a mixed programme or are we meditating all weekend on our own?'

'The programme is very, shall I say, fluid. It is thought that there are only two motivators of human action, pleasure and pain. Here we try to align them, but it is up to each member of the group to decide what activities they want to engage in.'

Still no help. 'What kinds of things have previous groups done during their retreat?'

Sarah could see Santosh behind the monk getting very agitated. 'Madam, I think we need go. Is long ride back.'

'All groups use the time to break down sexual barriers and perceived 'norms'. Discover what it feels like to be free from constraints, shame, guilt and other negative emotions that societies have around sex, sexual orientation, group sex and promiscuity. What form that takes depends on the individual group. There is no 'curriculum' as such.'

Sarah wasn't sure she'd heard right. She looked to Santosh. He had his eyes closed and was shaking his head.

'I see ... Well... that's very interesting.'

During this discourse they had been observed by several men who 'happened' to either walk past or sit nearby.

Santosh stood up. 'Madam. Is late.'

'Yes, Santosh. Thank you... I'd forgotten we agreed to go to the Zoo on the way back,' she lied.

Turning to the monk she bowed and pressed her hands in *Namaste*. 'Thank you so much for the tour. It's given me a lot to think about.'

Second Taste

He bowed back and they hastily took their leave.

Outside the gate Sarah bent double with suppressed laughter. She realised she'd been the only woman in there and kept remembering the men stalking her, popping their heads up like ducks in a firing range.

Thinking she was in pain Santosh asked, 'Is Madam all right?'

His look of concern sent her off into gales of laughter.

When they subsided she asked, 'Did you know about that place?'

He fidgeted before answering, 'Yes, Madam.'

'Why didn't you tell me?'

He shrugged, wobbled his head and said, 'I not sure.' Hesitating, he looked at the ground. 'Think maybe you want.'

'No, Santosh, it's not what I want. Is that what you were all discussing in the office?'

He looked up and nodded. 'They say you *badheshi*, it you *dharma*. But I must look after you.' He scowled at the retreat. 'Many, many bad men there.'

Moving to the archway he retrieved their bikes. Sarah took hers from him with a smile.

'Thanks.'

Santosh cocked a leg over his and turned to face her. With his bum parked on the worn saddle and one foot on the pedal, he beamed at her then winked. 'I glad you no want.'

She chuckled, tentatively climbed aboard the bike and followed him down the hill.

badeshi – foreigner   dharma – fate/way of being

Second Taste

I've been involved with writing in one form or another for most of my life and find inspiration in the world around me. In 1997 I changed my career of teacher and senior manager of community education in a high school and went as a volunteer with VSO to a placement in Nepal. This experience was a turning point and provided the inspiration for *Enlightenment* and material for my second novel, *Monsoons and Marigolds*. Prior to this placement the bulk of the work I had published was academic/educational, but in 2000 I embarked on an MA in Creative Writing at Northumbria University and started taking my poetry and prose seriously.

I have had poems published in anthologies and small press magazines like *Lookout, First Time, Southlight, Fankle, New Voices* (Federation of Writers, Scotland) and *Poetry Scotland* as well as on websites and e-zines and one of my poems won third prize in the Scottish Association of Writers *Write Down South* poetry competition. I have self-published two poetry pamphlets of my published poems, *The Language of Crows* and *A Suggestion of Bones*, and another, *Between Lands*, which was a collaboration of new work with fine art photographer Elliot Nichol. Short stories have been short listed by BBC Radio 4, won or were highly commended in competitions and one won an award from the Scottish Centre for Writing. Two novels, *In Desolate Corners, Shadows Crouch* and *Monsoons and Marigolds*, are self-published and available from Amazon.

Facebook: Kriss Nichol Writer
https://aninvisiblewoman.wordpress.com

Escaping Sephora

by Moomal Ahmed

Sephora is overrated.

That is my motto is on my fourteenth birthday.

So, help me Lord, when the other girls claim to be esteemed Sephora buyers, I hunch up my conspicuously mended skirts and, with feigned haughtiness, inform them that the brand they pursue so desperately is nothing but an illusion. 'Inept quality,' I announce to the gormless gaggle, 'behind a deceptive image.'

You, dear Lord, rub me with cheaper balms, to whiten further my pale skin and accentuate the right bones, the right curves for my job. The liquid in the black tin does wonders when diluted: it makes a woman out of a child and turns ungainliness to grace. That is all the compound asks for. 'Let them touch, let them forget, let them relax.' Sabrina has us recite this every evening before we leave. So while phony little princesses paint themselves freely with 'better' liquids, I swim deep in my own concealers, whitewashing here and coating there until I am satisfied the red marks on my neck – 'the marks of individuality' as Sabrina calls them – are obscured, and my countenance finally passes the Sephora test.

Then I go to school on my birthday. Why didn't you tell me it is a sin in the compound?

'Yo Camilla, you throwin' us a pardy or what?'

'C'mon, Camilla. Be a sport and give us a pardy to remember.'

Sabrina said once: be non-responsive unless they tell you to respond. None of those asking me questions ever specify that they want me to respond. Such conflicted signals. They think I'm impaired of my senses; I think I'm rule-abiding. Sabrina instructs me not to respond; you command me not to mislead. But lack of response misleads – it misled the people at school.

Alpha and Beta chased me for months. To think my cheaper liquids would entice them! Eventually, Sabrina's damned rules drove them away. I never could say that to her face – that her rules were big, fat pieces of damnation – but I liked attention at school. No, I'll rephrase that: I liked *their* attention. Add hypocrisy and lack of modesty to the list of faults you must punish me for. Alpha went back to leading and Beta to implementing his orders about 'which chicks to select' and 'which academic nonsense to bunk'. And I got back to part-time school, part-time compound.

September brought Alpha and Beta back. What they want is a pardy. I don't know what they mean by 'pardy'. I think it's similar to the 'partays' that happen in the compound every week. Alpha and Beta speak differently. They're American. Man F was American. And Man H. Sabrina hates Americans, says they're 'lustful hypocrites'. I think they aren't all that bad. Man F and Man H were actually akin to all the other men. Only they spoke funny. Like Alpha and Beta. Prastitute, not prostichute. Pardy, not partay. If they're the same words, then Alpha and Beta can't have their pardy without Sabrina's permission. She appoints only the best of us for such occasions: Jade, Fanny, Rose. Not Candy, never Candy. She says Candy is too torn between school and compound. She says Candy might be dismissed soon if she doesn't learn balance and isn't grateful enough.

'Yo Camilla, you throwin' us a partay or what?'

'C'mon, Camilla. Be a sport and give us a partay to remember.'

No, Alpha. No, Beta. Camilla doesn't do partays.

I wonder if Candy's response rule applies to Camilla. Do you allow me to break it once?

'No partay. No pardy. Sociology. Math. Math. Break. Math. No time for partay. No time for pardy.'

Second Taste

Alpha and Beta wear the same expression. That's the expression the compound wore when Sabrina sent me to school. You tell me. You're a know-it-all, aren't you? Or was it all-knowing. I forget which. Man F told me my English was horrible. Nice word. Horrible.

'You speak funny, girl. It's P-A-R-T-Y,' Alpha informs me.

'Okay. No P-A-R-T-Y. Sociology. Math. Math. Break. Math,' I correct myself. They laugh. I smile. Thank you, Lord, for making them laugh. I swear to you now: no more responding until told. Only smiling.

'Retard. Although, do give us a chocolate. It is your birthday after all.'

I blink.

Sabrina orders us to always comply with their wishes. If they tell you to stand, you stand. If they tell you to bend, you bend. Those are Candy's rules. I only remember Candy's rules right now. So I hand two of the five chocolates I got from Sabrina yesterday because I did my job well – I didn't respond and I complied with wishes – to Alpha and Beta.

'Dude, did she seriously just give us chocolates?'

'I think she doesn't have the moves for the game, man. Hey, you!' Beta goes along with Alpha's mood. That's his job. 'Change your name from Camilla to Weirdo.'

Still no new rules. Only Candy's rules. Comply. As Alpha and Beta leave, I work through my daily list. Sociology. Math. Math. Break. Eat the remaining three chocolates and lick the wrappers because I don't usually do my job that well and it's better to savour them than to waste the little melted parts. Math. School is over. I step out.

As I walk, I don't step on the cracks in the street tiles. It's a nice game. The other game I like is hide-and-seek. But Sabrina forbids it. Once when I hid, nobody found me till after midnight. My customers had to wait so long they eventually left. The compound was furious. She wastes her time in school and never does her job, they said. She's no good, they said. That's when I got my first flogging. Sabrina says you are always watching, so I pleaded to you and tried to convince you that I would never play hide-and-seek again. But you're a hard person to convince. Of course you're not a person; you're a Being, the category of which I cannot phrase. I did tell you that my vocabulary in English is limited. Long story shortened, I only play avoid-the-crack now.

Tile. Tile. Crack.

Oh, I stepped on it!

You knew that would happen, didn't you?

It's my last crack anyway. I've reached the limit of Camilla. She ends here, at the grey crossroads sign. I call it the CC Switch Limit. It's very creative; see, it switches from Camilla to Candy. I'm Camilla. I step once. Now I'm Candy. Step back, Camilla. Step forward, Candy again. It's fascinating really. But it's hard too; switching always has been for me.

I walk forward. Shoulders straight, curves thrust out. Candy is harder than Camilla is. Finally I reach the compound.

'You're late.' Sabrina waiting at the door always means I am.

'Sorry.'

That is something I didn't learn from Sabrina. You like it though, don't you? You consider apologizing for mistakes a good action. 'If I hurt others, give me the strength to repent.' You should love me more than the rest of them at the compound. None of them love you back; they love their jobs. It's just me. Probably Sabrina too, but some days she directs obscenities at you. That's another good word. Obscenities. Man H used them a lot, said he got 'carried away'. He said I was so well-nourished that my work quality reflected it. I made sure to remember that: he used obscenities because I was nourished and did my job well. That earns me chocolates.

'Tell me about your day, Candy.'

'Weirdo,' I say. It sounded different when Beta said it.

'What?'

'Not Candy. Weirdo. New name,' I tell Sabrina, expecting her to be appreciative. But instead, she gets furious. Her eyebrows are knitted together and her eyes are a dark red furnace, reminding me of that time I played hide-and-seek. Her eyes disturb me. They're frightening. Can you do me a favour right now? I know that you hold the most power in the universe. So can you make her forget she is angry? Make her happy again please.

'Well, aren't you an ungrateful little swine!'

I guess you can't.

'I've told you time and again that you should feel indebted for the privileges that you have gotten. You go to school, Candy, not to meddle yourself with the useless As and Bs they teach there but to speak proper English. It's good for business. We send you to learn the better phrases and the appropriate pronunciation. And you learn wrong words and unnecessary nonsense and call yourself Weirdo.' Sabrina is raging today. She might even slap me. My hands quiver. I want to tell her I only listened to her orders, that I complied. But I don't. Talking back brings the flogger. You didn't save me from the flogger last time; you won't save me this time. Only I can save myself.

'You have been cared for, Candy. Cared for and nourished. Your scrawny body has grown and your lips have become plump. You can bend and crouch and receive occasional beatings without your bones cracking. You have been nourished with good health and all the privileges a woman can desire. Feel glorious when you see those shapeless, aimless women strolling down aisles. You have one aim here – to please. And you have been nourished to achieve it.'

'I have been nourished.' Nourished is a difficult word. Different to 'horrible' and 'obscenities'. I don't like 'nourished'.

'Never let me see you be thankless again. I don't want to flog sense into you. Get ready, you're going to work at the partay tonight.'

'P-A-R-T-Y?'

'It's the only way of teaching you. Today isn't personal. It's public. A show. Be proud and tell the world you are blessed.'

'Partays are scary.'

Sabrina suddenly raises a hand above me. I cower.

Camilla tells me to stand up straight. Candy says cower. You have nourished Candy. And you hold the most power. I listen to Candy.

'Don't question me. Go doll yourself up for the guests.'

I stare at my bottle of liquid on which I scribbled 'Sephora' in grubby handwriting two days back, hoping to con myself into thinking that my birthday make-up was expensive, real make-up. It will need to be wiped off by alcohol, a nail polish remover or something.

Sabrina leaves. I stare at her.

Is she right? Do you favour Candy over Camilla? Why? Has Camilla sinned? I try my best not to make her sin. When I come and meet you one day after I'm old and no longer appealing and cast out of the compound, I'll attempt to explain. If Camilla is the sinner, guide her. She loves you more than Candy does. Most of all, she is grateful. She lives in the fancy that she is nourished more than her alter ego.

Second Taste

I don't think you're listening. You have so many people to listen to. Fanny and Rose say I don't complete my tasks so I'm not very important. I need to remove the pretend Sephora caption, doll up for the P-A-R-T-Y, restrict my dialogues, and never again use the American pronunciation that customers find too ugly and vulgar (except if or when Man F and Man H return for my services).

'Candy, you have customers.'

I start somewhat blatantly. Alpha and Beta in the compound is a unique sight. Camilla and Candy bump and muddle their groceries. They're tied together for some time now. I wonder if Camilla gets all her groceries back; she may forget bits of the entire list, bits that'll serve as memories of an accidental encounter. CC Switch Limit may just be off-route. An oxymoron may live in harmony. It's a prospect.

But there will always be starker differences.

'Hi, Candy. I hope you make today worth my while,' Alpha says. His permanent grin widens. 'You look just like someone from my school. Her name's Camilla.'

No, I don't.

You didn't nourish Camilla.

Lord, I repent for not realizing your favours.

~~~~~~~~~~~~~~

The author is an Economics student from Pakistan paying uncommon attention to the workings of society and subsequently writing about them.

She is into literature and journalism and believes that humans can write and express their way into a better society.

Done

by Thomas MacColl

'I'm going to have a wee biscuit, are you sure you don't want anything just now?'

'Nope... no thanks. Thanks.'

Speaking distractedly, he stirred two of five pots with a hurried, scraping motion, added a little water to one, sighed with relief and placed his hands on his hips, sighed impatiently, moved a lid from the smallest into a colander resting in the joint-second-largest, and threw a tea towel dramatically over one shoulder. There was a pot on each ring of the hob, plus one sitting in an oven tray of steaming water on a wire cooling rack with a hand-blender standing upright in it.

'You know... this will be ready in a few minutes' he remarked.

'Yes, and it looks great. I am going to have to have a biscuit or *something* now Tim, I am. I'm sorry, but I'm losing my mind with hunger here. Just going to eat one of these.'

'Sure, sure. Ten or fifteen minutes it'll be, that's all, then I'll put the potatoes in and they'll only take an hour, but it'll be less than that because, eh, they never really take as long as...'

'Thanks Tim, really, for doing all this. I'll just be over here, I've got this chapter to be working on anyway. Give me a shout if I can do anything.'

'All right, okaaaaaay – what next? What next? Hmm, I didn't peel these potatoes before the par-boi –'

'Can I do anything to help?'

'Hmm? Oh, no – I'm OK, really love, I think I've got it all, I'm just going to peel these and there's nothing else to be doing in the

Second Taste

meantime, I'll just keep stirring the roux while I'm peeling, and the oven's going to ping when the pastry's ready to come out, so then I'll –'

'Tim, I'm just going to put my, ah, headphones in, if that's OK with you?'

'Yup, sure thing – OK love, you do that – I'll get on with this peeling.'

Sweeping a large glass bowl from a deep drawer, he shimmied it onto a corner of the counter surface, wiggling a clearing through a copse of bottles, tubs and spoons with pooling and congealing juices of various colours in their bases. A displaced jar of whole peppercorns tumbled to the ground two feet to his left, but only a small scattering looked to have been shaken free, and the glass didn't sound like it had broken, so he tossed it towards the bottom of the to-do list. Becoming aware of the jumble of items this list comprised, each broadcasting its individual distress signal, was a thrilling and anxious experience. The skin across his ribcage tingled and tightened and he looked around with apprehension and pride. He bent over the glass bowl, took a new potato in his left hand and a peeler in his right, and set to stripping it.

He was roused from his reverie by a rustling at his shins. He started, and peered down. 'Hey' he heard, and Sarah's crown came into focus, then her hand gripping the counter. 'Just getting the oatcakes out, I'm sure there was still a packet in here somewhere.' She was hunkered down with her face and right arm deep in the cupboard, but now emerged triumphant and rose up, before slinking behind him. 'Can I just get into the fridge here and grab the cheese? Thanks.' He stared at her as though confused, and then at the pile of tiny brown potatoes to his left, which seemed hardly smaller than it had when he last looked. 'I've finished the draft of my conclusion, but Martin's emailed me with some notes on the last chapter now, so I'm going to go back over that. Can I get you a drink or something, chef?' His brow furrowed, and for a moment they each thought that he was about to burst into tears, but a shrill flurry of beeps erupted from behind him and he whirled round and opened the roaring oven. While he grabbed his gloves and peered into the glow, she snuck a knife from the drawer behind him and padded back to the table.

Finally tearing the last crescent of skin from the last potato, he gasped sharply and realised his jaw was throbbing from clenching. His hands were numb, but looking at them showed a fluffy, starchy coating, which may have been the cause of that symptom. He stumbled to the tap, rinsed them frantically, dried them on the least damp of the seven dishtowels within reach, and breathed again, deeper and slower. Now he sauntered back to the potatoes, removed the oven tray which had been in to get hot, poured a little olive oil, making it buck, and tossed the potatoes in; they sizzled as they made contact. He gave them some salt, pepper, a little dried chilli and pinches of various herbs, and tumbled them all around before placing them back in the middle shelf and closing the oven door with a flourish.

He checked his watch. 9.37pm – not too bad, not too bad, was it? Continental timings. The potatoes would be ready he supposed just a bit after 10, 10ish, and then that should pretty much be it; the quiches were mini, so wouldn't take as long as, you know, a big one. For now, he was going to have a seat. Just for a minute.

As his body surrendered to the sofa, relief coursed through him. With sudden largesse, he called out, 'Hey, Sarah. Well done on finishing your draft. Really, that's amazing, you're a genius. This meal is in your honour. How's it going over there?'

She looked up, took off her glasses and smiled softly at him. 'Hey, thank you. I'm doing all right, pretty well. I can't really believe it's there – four years I've been working on this. Of course Martin will have to check it over, and I know he didn't like some of the stuff I handed in last year, but he's been happy with me recently, so…'

'That's great Sarah. You want a drink or something? Clink together to celebrate?'

Second Taste

'You know, I'd love a drink. Just... don't really want to start drinking on an empty stomach, you know?'

'Well, you had some things to eat just now didn't you? I know I'm still cooking, but it won't be long...'

'Tim, it's nearly 10 pm, and I haven't had anything since a sandwich at lunchtime, apart from a custard cream and a couple of stale oatcakes. And I've just basically finished my thesis. I am seriously considering putting in a pizza. Call it a starter.'

'I don't – uh, you don't need to have a pizza, do you? This'll be ready in about half a, around about 10, or – it won't be too long. Are you really that hungry?'

'Yes, Tim. I am actually.'

He stared into her eyes for a long few seconds; his fingers started to twitch. Then he jumped up, darted round, gave a stir and a shoogle and balanced one precarious pile of dishes on top of another. No time to get into that. Must make a start on dessert. First, though, he had an idea. He opened the freezer quietly, but shuffled his feet noisily, and removed the ice cube tray. He put a few cubes each in two glasses as secretly as he could, wincing as they snapped and scraped at each other. He ducked into the thin corner cupboard, placed the crackling glasses on the floor and shuffled his slippers again as he poured Campari into each glass. With a flourish he emerged from behind the counter, and held out the glasses. She stared at him drily and, after a moment's hesitation, he placed them both on the table. 'Tim.' She didn't touch the glass. 'Is this meal going to be ready to start eating within the next... 20 minutes?'

'Em, well... I could put out some...'

'Will we be able to sit down and eat before 11pm? Should I set the table?'

'Sarah, you know, you can't rush these –'

'I can rush a pizza, I can rush it in ten minutes. It'll be done before you've, I don't know, pureed the peas or whatever, and I'll probably be hungry again by the time this is ready anyway.'

'Sarah, I really would appreciate it if – oh, you're just going to – I've put a lot of, well, I don't want to end up eating all this on my own! And I need all the shelves in there.'

The oven roared again briefly, she slipped out from behind the counter and regained her seat. He furrowed his brow at her, grabbed a large plastic jug, scooped a handful of peas from a brown paper bag, and noisily extracted the hand blender from the drying rack. The blitzing proved a little awkward. First they powdered, and he splashed in some water; then he regretted water's blandness and added the juice of half a lemon and two tablespoons of olive oil. Next they became too slushy, so he reluctantly banged around the cupboard for an acceptable re-thickener, sighing all the while. He was just about to blend in a tablespoon of cornflour when she nipped back through, took a plate, had the oven door open and shut before he could press the blender button, and was at the table with a steaming pizza. 'Would you like a bit, Tim?' she called over. He pressed the blender button.

*

The potatoes, upon turning, were well on their way, starting to crisp up nicely. The mini-quiche filling turned out to be just the right amount; he filled the pastry cases and slipped them in below the potatoes. He plunged his grateful hands into a steaming basin of soapy water and picked away at the edges of his mound of dirty dishes. Between further checks on the oven and the mousse setting in the fridge, he heard Sarah give her enter key a bash of satisfaction and pick up the glass he had left her. He dried his hands slowly on a fresh tea towel, raised his own glass to her behind her back, leaned on the edge of the counter and asked, 'Hey love, do you still have a piece of that starter to spare?'

Second Taste

Having grown up in Fife, I have lived in Edinburgh for the past decade, and have been actively involved in the literary world of the city throughout my time there. A keen writer and reader since childhood, my primary interest in writing is short fiction, although I also write poetry (both individually and collaboratively) and non-fiction. I studied English Literature at the University of Edinburgh between 2007 and 2011. In 2013 my short story *Timer* was selected as part of the Edinburgh International Book Festival's annual Story Shop event, giving me the chance to read my work in the Spiegeltent in Charlotte Square; I was shortlisted for Story Shop again in 2014. I have also read my fiction as part of 2014's *Is 5* event at Main Point Books. In 2017 I was the recipient of the Mairi Hedderwick Travel Writing Bursary at Moniack Mhor, Scotland's Creative Writing Centre, gaining a place on a week-long course at the centre. In addition to my own prose writing, my other main literary outlet has been a collaborative poetry project with Ed Smith (which can be viewed at ed-and-tom.tumblr.com).

Rosie

by Matt Gibson

The click of the morphine syringe chimed the hour and Samuel Entwistle sank into the mattress, cocooned in the warmth of the starched white sheets. The drip bubbled in the dark and the pump whispered. His hand, fragile veins pierced with plastic tubing, was coddled in velvet. His breathing softened, his eyes open with dreams.

He was alone in the room, alone with the morphine, alone with sting of detergent, alone with the sluggish wall clock, alone with the line that fed him liquid nutrition and the catheter that carried it away.

Alone with the stage four cancer that had spread from liver to lung to bone, that fed quietly on his ailing, aching body, that let nothing go to waste.

Laughter from the corridors and the rattle of trolleys, the nursing shift changing for the night. The dim orange glow of the street light casting its nuclear haze across the floor. The tick, tick, tick of the sluggish clock.

The morphine stirred. The smell of flowers. The gentle descent of Pachelbel's Canon, the third violin ghosting in before the counter voice of the viola. Belinda, a tiny wine stain on her wedding dress, joining him on the town hall dance floor. The popping of corks and the clinking of glasses. Laughter and hope.

The door opened a fraction. Sam looked over without raising his head. Bright white light dazzled from the corridor.

'Mr Entwistle?' It was Christine, the ward nurse.

He wanted to reply but the strings were in full flow now, the dancing fluid and alive.

Second Taste

'Is everything okay, Mr Entwistle?'

He smiled, his head bobbing on his pillow.

'I'll take that as a yes.' Gentle as a shadow she lowered a box to the ground, just inside the door. She placed a finger to her lips. 'Our secret – don't tell anyone. It's really not allowed. You rest peacefully, now.'

She closed the door and he closed his eyes. Applause, sunlight through the high town hall windows, bright beams catching on Belinda's eyes, her cheekbones, her hair.

The drip clicked. The temperature dropped and the music faded. A needle burned high in his arm, the liquid feed keeping him alive. Alive enough to hear the clock tick on.

He felt it in his feet, then his fingers. The pain, the burning, stabbing pain. He bit his lip. His cheeks were wet with tears.

*

Belinda had died in the night five years earlier. A heart attack. Painless, the doctor said, she would have known nothing about it. A fine way to go.

They had been married for 50 years and on the day of the funeral Sam resolved to starve himself to death.

It wasn't easy under the watchful eye of the villagers. They had instinctively taken turns to visit him, pretending the half mile trip to the isolated cottage was a natural part of their daily routines.

So every Wednesday Sam dragged himself into town to 'stock up' on food, on bread, soups and meats that would never make it to the table. He may have been thinner and weaker on each visit, but the rouse was enough to deceive the well-wishers. 'At least he's looking after himself' was their doubtful refrain.

A month after the burial and Sam set off on the weekly ritual. He passed the fading roses in the garden. He closed the front gate and walked along the puddled track as rain dripped from his jacket collar and into the front of his shirt. Thick mud groaned at his every step and the wind picked up across the dull fields, whipping cold spray from the hedgerows.

He stopped at the rusted gate to adjust his hood. He could taste the frost in the air, the sky a dark canopy.

He paused, rubbing his ears. He held his breath and squinted in concentration. A squeal had cut through the beat of the rain, a soft cry. Sorrowful and yearning.

He frowned and kicked at the bushes. Silence. The wind howled. He buttoned his jacket and carried on into town.

An hour's wandering from shop to shop. An hour of small talk and of buying unwanted supplies. And finally, the walk back. The journey home was always easier, his task for the week done, his face shown, wagging tongues silenced.

Water dripped from overhanging branches, but the worst of the rain had passed. The sky was indifferent and anaemic.

He stopped by the gate, leaned his back against the rusted frame. Crows called out from the woodland. A cow bellowed in response. He heard the squeal again.

He scratched his chin and frowned. He crouched down by the ditch and pushed the damp grass aside. He peered behind a root.

The body of a cat lay on a small rocky ledge, an inch above a stream of rainwater. Fragile blue eyes looked back at him, then immediately away. A mewl.

He touched the cat, her body cold. She lay on her side, belly exposed to the elements. The kitten buried its face in her side and kneaded her fur, its paws frantic as it attempted to suckle. It looked up and called again.

Second Taste

Shapes in the water. He kneeled lower. Two more kittens were beneath the surface, lifeless, their fur moving with the icy flow.

Sam reached for the survivor. It hissed and backed away.

'Come on, little one,' he said. He took a pint of milk from his shopping bag and poured some onto his fingers. He held them towards the kitten. It inched forward and took tentative laps at his skin.

'You sad little thing,' he said. 'You poor, sad little thing.'

As it licked his one hand he placed the other beneath its belly and lifted it up. It cried and writhed in protest, feeble scratches from unformed claws. But he held it to his breast, covering it with the warmth of his jacket, and it calmed.

'I think you'd better come with me,' he whispered.

He switched on the heater in the living room and the house warmed for the first time since the funeral. He placed down bowls of milk then boiled a chicken breast, cutting the fillet into tiny morsels. He sat with the door closed while the kitten ate furtively in the corner. He went through the boxes of clothes, destined for the charity shop, and took out the softest material. He shaped it inside a basket. He turned on the radio, quiet classical music. He searched through drawers for the balls of wool Belinda had never quite got around to knitting with.

Later, when the kitten was hiding away, he went back to the farmer's gate. He collected the mother and her offspring and carried them home. He buried them in the garden that afternoon.

The kitten slept through the ceremony. She was a girl and he called her Rosie.

The months passed and the weekly shopping trips became daily. He ate and he fed. Colour returned to his cheeks and strength to his limbs. The whispered sympathies in town disappeared, replaced with joking and laughter over a pint at the Seven Bells.

Mrs Simpson, on one final fraudulent errand which happened to pass his cottage, was delighted to find him in the front garden, watering the flowers. Rosie scampered about his legs and darted at sparrows.

He joined the village bowling club and made readings in church. He signed up for courses and learned foreign languages, parroting stock phrases in an alien voice as Rosie slept on his lap. He resumed work on the book that deep down he knew he would never finish.

Rosie would wait by the window when he went out and rumble with purrs on his return. She was with him in the bedroom when he slept and in the study when he read.

She was with him a year on, the frightened wet kitten turned glossy black cat. She was with him three years later when the blizzards came and the pair spent the winter huddled in front of the fireplace.

She was with him four years later when the doctor's letter arrived: further tests required. She nuzzled at his feet when he returned from the hospital, paper bags of medicine beneath his arm.

She lay on the bed when the district nurse took to visiting and never complained that he no longer played with her in the garden.

She was with him when a place was found in the nearest hospice. He kissed her for a final time as the ambulance arrived.

*

Sam wiped the tears from his face and glanced up at the sluggish clock. His joints were locked tight and it felt as if acid was gnawing through his sides. He bit into his lip again, hard enough to draw blood had his body got any to spare.

He dug his nails into his palms and stared at the morphine syringe. The streetlight flickered, the strange box by the door.

The corridor was silent, the light beneath the door long out. No one to disturb him. He had been in the hospice for a fortnight, and in a ward dormitory until two days earlier.

The luxury of a private room that came with an unspeakable price.

He heard the ticking of the clock. He heard the dull tapping of his heart.

He heard a squeal. Yearning, sorrowful.

He squinted towards the door. A shadow in the orange haze. The soft pad of feet.

A thump on the bed. He reached forward, touching Rosie's soft fur. She meowed then purred as he rubbed the back of her neck. She walked up to his face and put her nose against his damp cheek.

He stroked her as she lay next to him, her fur by his face, her paws on his neck. The plastic in his hand brushed against her tail.

Gently he reached over her body and fumbled at the tubes. He pulled the tape loose. The morphine IV came out easily from the back of his hand, a drop of glistening liquid falling onto the sheets from the needle's tip. The food line was more awkward, high up his arm, and he had to strain his shoulder to coax it free.

He smelt flowers and heard the first quiet bars of Pachelbel's Canon. He closed his eyes. Bright beams of sunlight caught on Belinda's eyes, her cheekbones, her hair. Rosie scampered about his legs and darted at sparrows.

Second Taste

Matthew Gibson was born and brought up in London, where he lives with his partner and two cats. He studied English literature at university where he developed a love of the short story form. Now, several years later, he has decided to try his hand at his own.

Mirabelle

by Susanna Callaghan

At the age of twelve, Mirabelle hadn't a clue what she wanted to be when she grew up; she only knew that what she needed most of all was to find True Love. This would arrive in the form of a prince like the ones she found in the fairy stories she read and the romantic films she watched, a prince she brought to life in vivid, delicious daydreams where he was her very own happy-ever-after, come to capture her heart, nourish her soul and complete her in every way.

Mirabelle's perfect man was tall, darkly good-looking, silent and mysterious. As time passed, he evolved from 'tall, dark and handsome' into a passionate, brooding, dauntless character, dangerous and unpredictable with others, but always gentle with her, sharing his innermost thoughts. Together they surmounted all kinds of hazards: sometimes she was a princess in peril and he would brave unbelievable danger to rescue her; more often she was the heroine to his hero: pirates roaming the seven seas, adventurers discovering lost civilisations. His name went through variations too, but like his looks, eventually it stabilised: he was Valentine.

Mirabelle attended an all-girls high school, which meant that her adventures with Valentine were undisturbed by any actual boys (her irritating younger brother didn't count). In some of her daydreams, her father, who was often away on business trips, was a king, who would have been a wonderful, loving parent if he hadn't had to go off fighting wars or seeing to various troubles in his kingdom.

*

At the age of fifteen, Mirabelle's best friend was a quiet girl with long brown hair called Alison. They shared classes and as they came to trust each other, they shared their secrets too. Mirabelle told Alison about Valentine; Alison spoke of her crush on Mark, an actor in a popular TV series. They stayed over at each other's house, making up stories in which they set out with Mark and

Valentine (who also became close friends) on a perilous adventure that ended with the world being saved and, more importantly, them in their lovers' arms. In Mirabelle's opinion, Mark, with his fair hair, blue eyes and kindliness, was an ideal partner for Alison; but Valentine was better in every respect, and when they kissed their pillows, his response was far more passionate.

*

At seventeen, Mirabelle had never been kissed by anyone else. But that year, with tremulous curiosity, she let a boy at the youth club have a go at Christmas: horrified at the reality of it – slobber, spots and hot, smelly breath – she pushed him away and ran home. As she grew older, there were other kisses, marginally better, but nothing likely to tempt her away from Valentine; compared to him, the boys she met were so gauche, and inevitably drunk before the evening was out. Amazingly, some were surprised or indignant when she rejected them.

University, where she studied Spanish, brought wider choices, but still no one who came anywhere close to Valentine. They were boys, that's all – not a trace of charm or romance, and though Mirabelle attracted many, she became adept at sweeping them all into the Friend Zone. But it mattered little because Valentine was still with her, as dark, mysterious and attractive as ever, appearing several times a day to sweep her off her feet and whirl her into adventure.

*

She turned nineteen. As part of her course, she was to spend a year at the Universitad Autónoma de Madrid. *Wow*! This was her immediate thought on arriving: all the men (or at least the ones she noticed) were brown-eyed, tanned and handsome. Ripe and ready for her to conquer their heart.

Jaime was one of them: tall, confident and charming, saying and doing the right things, romancing her utterly. Everything British men were not. Mirabelle fell into his arms, totally in love for the first time in her life. Jaime loved her too, so of course they would eventually get married. The problems to overcome, such as which country they'd live in, or their differing backgrounds and beliefs, were trivial, because love, as everyone knows, conquers all.

The only hitch was that this meant an end to her tryst with Valentine, but Mirabelle accepted that it was time to embrace the real world. She therefore fixed a date with him in a meadow of daydream flowers, and as they walked hand in hand, she broke the news.

'Valentine, my dearest, you'll always be a part of me...'

She had no need to say more – he understood. And though his dark, brooding eyes were filled with sorrow, he accepted.

'Jaime is very like you, you know. I think he may even *be* you. Just a bit more... real. If you see what I mean.'

With perfect grace, he murmured that he did.

'This, then, is the last time we can meet. I must leave now, Valentine. Farewell...'

Valentine bent to kiss her hand. 'Farewell, my love.' Then, his smile heartbreakingly sad, he dematerialised.

*

Three months later, Jaime ended the relationship. When she pressed him to know why, he said it wasn't working out – they were too different. To Mirabelle, this was impossible: something – or someone – must have come between them. She begged him to reconsider: nothing could defeat their love, they were destined to be together. Exasperated, Jaime came out with the truth: she was clingy, stifling, immature, possessive... the list went on.

Mirabelle cried her eyes sore. Driven to distraction by her endless moping and moaning, her friends told her to get a grip. Unhappier than ever, she turned to food and drink. Somehow, she got to the end of her year in Madrid; on returning to England she came to a decision...

*

'Wow, Belle, you look wonderful. Toned, tanned – and the slimmest you've ever been! Not that you were ever fat, of course.' Alison gave her a hug. 'It's lovely to see you!'

'You look great too. It's been such a long time!'

'I miss the old days, you know. So much has happened since then.'

They were outside the British Museum. It brought back happy memories of their school visit when they were fifteen – they'd made up a story in which a suit of armour came alive and attacked them. Luckily, Mark and Valentine were on hand.

'Let's go to a café,' Alison said.

'A pub would be nicer.'

'A pub? We just want to sit and catch up.'

'Which we will. It's been ages! Come on, there's a good one just round the corner.'

They found a quiet corner at the back, and Mirabelle said, 'What are you having?'

'No, I'll get them. What's yours?'

'Oh, all right. Next round's on me, though. Tequila Sunrise. Thanks.'

When the drinks arrived, Mirabelle was astonished. 'A lemonade? Is that all?' She raised her glass. 'Cheers. Nothing like this to loosen you up before going out. Drinks are so expensive in clubs. If we get a few inside us now, we can have a lemonade when we get there.' She winked at Alison. 'Until we meet some guys.'

'What?' Alison drew back her head. 'I'm sorry, clubbing's not my scene, Mirabelle. And I don't drink. Besides, I want to get back by eleven.'

'What?' It was Mirabelle's turn to be shocked. 'Come on, Alison, live a little! We won't meet anyone *here*.'

'Fine. I'm not looking to meet anyone. It's you I wanted to see.'

'Of course. And I want to see you. But... there's more to life than boring old me. *Ruby Ruse* – the club I'm thinking of? The guys there... It's like picking cherries from a tree.'

'But can't we just...' Alison spread her hands. 'Look, I'm in a relationship, Mirabelle. Pete. I met him at Aberdeen. I'm sorry, I was going to write, then I thought I'd tell you in person. But I'm...' She shook her head, nonplussed. 'What's happened to you? You seem so different.'

'Really?' Mirabelle laughed – it came out more as a sneer. 'I grew up, that's what. Got rid of my stupid ideas. Decided to play the field and play it well. Right now I've got, let me see... there's Daniel and Lewis and Aaron. Not Harvey – I ditched him last week. All of them loaded, of course.'

Alison sat there gaping. 'But why? You used to be so... *we* used to be. Ok, we all grow up, but you've gone from one extreme to the other. How come?'

'Simple. I fell in love. And guess what? I got hurt. Men only want one thing, Alison. Fair enough – I'm perfectly happy to go along. But two can play at that game and I've not yet met a man who plays it better than me. '

'Oh, Belle, I'm so sorry. But one bad experience – you mustn't let that harden you.' Alison put her hand on Mirabelle's knee. 'I'm going to pray for you. It'll work out, you'll see.'

'Pray for me?' Mirabelle snorted. 'Why thank you! But I'd rather rely on myself than God. Where on earth did you get that nonsense from?'

'It isn't nonsense. Most of my friends at Uni are Christians. I've simply accepted Christ as my personal saviour and my life has a purpose now. He can be your saviour too. All you need do is let him.'

'No, Alison, hang on. That's not my kind of thing. Not at all. I suppose Pete is Christian too?'

'Yes, of course. Look, Mirabelle, why not give it a go? There's bound to be a Christian Union at Southampton. I'm not out to push it on you, it's just that you seem so lost. Go along and give it a try, you'll see. Whatever you're suffering, it can be healed.'

Mirabelle didn't answer. She felt as if a bag of cement was pressing down on her chest. She gulped the last of her tequila. 'I miss the happy times we had together.'

'Mmm. The stories. They were fun.'

A long, uncomfortable silence grew between them. Eventually Mirabelle, desperate for another drink, said, 'Yes. Well, look, it's been great seeing you again. We must keep in touch.'

'Of course.' Rather eagerly, Alison stood up. 'I'd love you to meet Pete…'

'Mmm, yes. Might be hard, though. Me in Southampton, you in Aberdeen…'

'Maybe for graduation?'

'Maybe.'

They hugged each other again, and Mirabelle watched her friend walk away before heading back to the bar.

*

Half way through her final year, Mirabelle turned twenty-one, and one of her boyfriends gave her twenty-one red roses. 'How sweet!' she said, and took a photo. The following week she dumped him; he was getting altogether the wrong idea.

Then an email arrived from Alison: *Mirabelle, we'd love it if you could come up to Aberdeen in the summer. Pete and I are graduating and not only that but we're getting engaged. We want to have a celebration with our closest friends and family. We haven't decided the date yet, but I just wanted to let you know. He proposed on St Valentines Day…*

She should have been happy. She should have called straightaway: *Alison, I'm so excited for you! Congratulations*! But instead, Mirabelle threw herself on the bed and wept. And kept on weeping till she fell asleep, at which point a gentle hand came to stroke her cheek, and a voice murmured softly, 'Poor thing…'

She looked up, astounded. 'Valentine!'

He said nothing, but his hand continued to soothe her. Never had he been more wonderful, his warm, brown eyes overflowing with a love that spilled into pools of gold around her. She wanted to take his hand, draw him closer, let him lie down beside her. But she couldn't. *Go back to him now*? She couldn't.

Valentine held her gaze for another long moment, his eyes fathomless. Then he turned and walked away.

*

Try as she might, Mirabelle couldn't concentrate. The role of the Soviet Union in the Spanish Civil War… What did that matter to anyone? She closed the book, not bothering to return it, and dragged herself out of the library to… what? Outside the library, everything was as pointless as inside. *That's the whole point of pointlessness. It's everywhere.* She stumbled across the campus, her features set in a grimace.

Second Taste

Ten days now since she'd received Alison's email, and she still hadn't answered. Shame on you, Mirabelle. Do it! But instead, she kept on walking, not registering anything, till eventually she found herself at Highfield Church.

For several minutes, she stood by the gate, head bowed. A passer-by might have thought she was praying, or absorbed in meditation. In truth, she was watching her tears fall on the pavement and thinking it was too late: whatever healing was inside the church, it wasn't the healing she needed.

'Come with me, Mirabelle. Come…'

How could she? There was only one way they could be together… And yet… when she considered what her life was without him…

That night, Valentine appeared again, waiting for her in an endless meadow of buttercups. He held out a hand and as Mirabelle reached to take it, gazing into eternal bliss, she knew her decision was right.

And they lived happily ever after.

Learn How To Fall

by Julian Cope

Mum threw me out, she did. Just like that.

Pushed me out. Actually *shoved* me onto the front porch.

I mean, I wasn't expecting her to do that. I hadn't done nothing wrong.

I hadn't done *nothing*!

I was just sitting there.

Waiting for dinner.

Suddenly she starts off at me, niggling me.

Took me by surprise, just pushing and shoving, like.

She never said a word at first, but I could see she meant business.

I made a kind of attempt at protest, but she simply ignored it.

It was too late, anyway. I was outside!

She gave one more push, so hard that I stumbled and tumbled to the ground.

That really brought me down to earth with a bump, I can tell you.

I wasn't hurt. Not much. Carefully I stood up and looked around.

She's standing there, glaring at me.

I open my mouth to ask 'Why?' but she shouts back at me: 'You be quiet! Just shut it!'

I didn't say nothing.

'You're not coming back in here! You just stay where you are.'

I didn't say nothing. I just wanted to cry. But I wasn't going to let her see.

Still she keeps on, going on at me.

'You're in big trouble now, so just watch out! Just you watch it!'

My heart was beating fast.

What had happened? Why did she do that?

I hated her.

I wanted her.

I wanted her to come to me and give me a cuddle, like before.

Like she always did.

But she just stands there, defiant. 'I'm warning you! Just belt up! Shut it!'

'Shut it!'

'Shut it!'

'Shut it, or else!'

'I said SHUT IT!'

I couldn't take much more of that, so I thought I'd better hop it.

I went around the other side of the hedge where she couldn't see me.

But I could still hear her.

'Your Dad will be home soon. He'll tell you. You listen to him!'

Second Taste

I'll stay where I am.

Maybe Dad will let me come home.

I'll sit here and wait.

What about the others? My sisters, my little brother?

They weren't doing nothing either.

Will she chuck them out as well?

Why me? What did I do?

I'm hungry.

It's getting dark. I'm cold.

What's that noise? I don't like it here.

Something moved.

I'm so hungry. When's dinner?

I'm scared.

There she goes again.

'Watch out! Your Dad's here. He'll tell you.'

I call out: 'Dad?'

'Be quiet, son.'

'But Dad…'

'I said *be quiet*!'

Something did move. In the bushes over there.

I can't see it.

Mum starts screaming again. Over and over.

Second Taste

Nothing moves now.

Except Mum and Dad, of course.

They're darting around all over the place.

'Back off!'

That was Dad.

'Back off! Piss off out of it!'

I'm scared.

I try to make myself small.

Smaller.

'Piss off!'

'Shit-face!'

'Hey, Shit-face! Over here!'

I never heard Dad swear like that before. Is he swearing at *me*?

Mum flies across to the tree behind me, rattling the branches.

'No. Over here, you great turd! Over here, Shit-whiskers!'

'Don't move, son!' That was Dad again. 'Keep still.'

Then he lands on the grass near the bushes.

He's hurt. His wing is broken. Oh, no! No! He's fallen over!

He's up again. Hobbling away.

'Can't catch me-ee! You great ugly bastard!'

Now he's airborne again!

I wish I could do that.

Second Taste

The commotion. It's so loud.

I'm scared. I've just done a poo. Couldn't help it.

The air is full of screams, and birds.

But it's only the two of them, Mum and Dad. They're everywhere!

Dad's on the ground once more, right by those bushes.

Shouting insults and taunting... someone.

But there's no-one there? Or is there?

I can't see anything.

It's getting really dark.

I'm hungry.

Second Taste

Julian Cope, a wartime baby in Derby, spent a significant part of his infancy sheltering in a small cot under the kitchen table (he was too young to remember the sirens and falling bombs). After grammar school he enjoyed a short spell as a trolleybus conductor, and hated an 11-year 'sentence' as a bank officer. Escaping in his early thirties he gained a Goldsmiths College diploma in Youth & Community Work, at a time the National Front were marching through the streets of South East London.

25 years' employment in Local Authorities saw him developing community activities in deprived neighbourhoods, training Council staff and volunteers, and auditing the quality of care provision. In 1982 he took a 7-year break, moving to Suffolk to open a restaurant in the centre of Bury St Edmunds. He is about to commence his 50th season refereeing adult amateur football.

But now he has caught the creative writing 'bug', having joined two local groups. This is his second short story to be published. There will be more; you ain't seen nuffin' yet!

Second Chances

by Parker McIntosh

Chad Hastings sat in his recliner before bed, his lips pursed in a conundrum. He was going to settle for another glass of wine, he knew that already, but what he really wanted was a beer. He remembered the days when a twelve pack in the fridge wouldn't last Friday night let alone the weekend, but ever since Myrtle went on her health craze his drinking habits changed.

He couldn't really argue with her. Back in college Chad had one of the best six-packs (abs, not beer) on campus, more due to a phenomenal metabolism than any kind of athletic rigor. But since graduating and indulging in the joy of a beer or ten after work his six-pack turned into a fleshy quarter-keg.

Myrtle hadn't complained about his figure. Lord knows she hadn't kept hers. Her muffin top he once thought almost looked cute bulged until her belly-button was indiscernible from belly rolls, her upper arms flapped like little bat wings when she walked, and the cellulite- well it wasn't pretty to see her in a bathing suit anymore.

But they lived their lives, he going to the office to do what he admitted was monkey work and she to the hospital where she registered new patients, letting each other degenerate into spherical masses of flesh in silent agreement that it was ok as long as they both did it.

And then Chad had his heart attack. That woke Myrtle up. Immediately their fridge transformed. Or rather their freezer emptied of microwaveable meals and the fridge filled up with more than just condiments. Suddenly there were green things, lots of them. The worst fight was over the beer.

Myrtle insisted he cut back on beer. 'It's empty calories and you're hurting your heart. Please! For me!'

And in respect of their marriage Chad consented. He agreed to no more than a six-pack per week. At first it had been hard, but after he figured out that Myrtle believed a glass of wine every day helps the heart it got easier. She read it somewhere on the internet. After downing a bottle in a night Chad realized wine did the trick just as well as beer. He had to get used to the acidic rush on his palate after the first sip, the non-carbonated bite. But he could feel it working on him. Like oil to a chain, the second and third glass loosened his brain.

He missed that metallic carbonated first twang of a Budweiser. He wanted it badly, but that meant getting up out of his recliner and walking all the way to the kitchen and enduring Myrtle's stare from the table where she did the Sudoku and Scramble in the New York Times as he pulled the long-neck out of the fridge. *You're killing yourself,* that stare would say. She would sigh just loud enough for him to hear and then it would be impossible to really enjoy the beer. It was so much easier to pour another glass of wine out of the already open bottle on the fold-out table next to him.

Charlie was asleep. That was a good thing because Chad felt his lips loosening and he might have told the boy what he really thought of his rat-tail. *He's only eight,* Myrtle had said. *Let him wear his hair how he wants to. He's too impatient to let it really grow.* But she had been wrong. Chad didn't even know where the kid found out about rat-tails but it had been over a year and despite asking on every trip to the barber, 'Aren't you tired of that old thing? It's gotta be a pain to wash in the shower,' or some other ploy to get him to chop it off, the hair remained. It now reached half-way down Charlie's back and Chad had to keep himself from giving it a firm *yank*! every time the boy passed. Once he had actually stuck his hand out and grabbed it but the mortifying and hungover memory of Charlie's face, confused more than hurt, stopped Chad from taking his second glass of wine until after the boy went to sleep.

Charlie had been a mistake. Chad admitted it though Myrtle never would. They'd tried to have kids right after the wedding, two months after college. They both had jobs, great benefits, they didn't see a better time. But no amount of unprotected humping could get her to conceive. Chad wondered why they'd even bothered using condoms in college. They accepted solitary life with each other and, as they both assumed was natural, stopped having sex except on birthdays. All of a sudden, a few weeks after she turned forty, Myrtle stopped getting her period.

'I think I might be pregnant,' she said at dinner. Chad had grunted. *She's putting one over me or she's finally lost it*, he thought.

'Are you sure it isn't... you know.' He swiped his hand across his neck in a rough approximation of *the end.*

'I'm not old enough for menopause,' she yelled, shoving her chair back and storming out of the kitchen. Chad thought he'd been funny.

Looking back on it Chad thought pregnancy hadn't been kind to Myrtle. Up until she had Charlie she'd gained weight but nothing she couldn't hide under a sweater. After gaining thirty pounds to pass a six-pound lump her body metamorphosed. Her breasts sagged and never perked up. Her gait turned to a waddle. They'd had sex three times since the boy was born and Chad didn't care to remember any of them.

Chad looked at the now nearly empty bottle of wine poking over his own fleshy bicep and wondered what was taking Myrtle so long. Usually after finishing the Sudoku and Scramble she came in to watch the end of whatever game he was watching and catch The Daily Show before they went to bed. It was one tradition they hadn't changed in years. 'Sudoku must be kicking her ass tonight,' Chad said loud enough he thought she could hear. He turned up the TV as The Daily Show started.

It wasn't all bad, Chad figured. The marriage and life thing. There had been vacations to the Outer Banks in North Carolina and more recently Disney World. They had anniversary limo rides to expensive dinners even he couldn't say weren't romantic. They'd made a good run of it, just in retrospect it all ran together in a mush of *how did I get so old.*

Chad looked down at his stomach and realized he couldn't see his knees. It was the first time he'd noticed. Below the bulge of his gut he could just see the tips of his toes sticking up covered by the gray-tipped white socks Myrtle bought him every year. They were the same style he'd worn through college. He wiggled his toes and laughed.

Myrtle really had taken the health kick seriously. Chad snuck lunches at McDonald's and had steaks with people he worked with whenever he could, but Myrtle stuck to her diet. She mentioned losing thirty-something pounds recently, Chad couldn't remember exactly, but the more he thought about it the more he realized she was starting to look good.

He hadn't noticed because it was such a gradual transformation but her shirts were hanging looser, her arms looked thinner. He wondered what she looked like under her shirt nowadays.

The wine reminded Chad how they used to shamelessly flirt in college when they were drunk. He couldn't remember the last time he'd snuck up behind her and grabbed her bottom affectionately. He was possessed with the urge to let her know he noticed she looked good. To show her he cared. *I'll throw out the Budweiser*, Chad thought. *She's having a rough time with Sudoku, it'll make her smile. Then I'll kiss her on the forehead and tell her I'll lose fifty pounds by Christmas. I'll start walking in the mornings tomorrow*! It was an easy promise to make on the dregs of a bottle of wine.

Chad struggled to his feet and was embarrassed by how hard his heart thumped. He left the empty wine bottle on the table and walked into the kitchen.

Myrtle was on her back on the floor. For a moment nothing registered. It was such an absurd picture seeing her flat on her back her eyes bulging, bug-like, out of her skull. And then Chad un-froze and ran to her.

He shook her, harder than he should have. *Not like the movies*, he thought. His mind was everywhere at once. *In the movies they say something. Her name.*

'Myrtle,' he said weakly, but he knew it was no use. Her shoulders already felt room temperature and stiff. He jerked away and fought down an acidic burp.

Chad called the police. He told them no, it wasn't an emergency, but his wife was dead. The words passed his lips like pudding. They plopped into the phone and sat in such an ugly silence he hung up.

Chad looked down at Myrtle, her whole body, and for the first time registered just how much of her college frame she'd recovered in the past year. Hiding behind a few crow's feet and worry-lines he could see the girl he met in English 101. She had green sparkling eyes, wore leggings and long shirts barely covering her butt that screamed *ask me out!* and every smile came with two dimples.

Her dimples. They were paralyzed on her grimace in a pained facsimile of former cuteness. Chad tried to press them away but they were stuck. Immortalized on her cheeks.

The police showed up with an ambulance. They were rough with him initially and in retrospect he probably should have told them how his wife died before hanging up but once they assessed the situation they became apologetic.

The paramedics took their time wheeling her out to the ambulance and turned the flashing lights off. No emergency now.

Somehow Charlie slept through the whole ordeal. Chad debated waking him up to follow the paramedics to the hospital but decided against it. He would take him to the funeral home, once they'd dressed her up nicely and put some makeup on her. Maybe they could take those damned dimples off her face.

The boy's going to need a mother figure.

Chad felt like he'd been slapped. His wife was hardly cold and he was already thinking about replacing her.

He's going to be even more lost than me when he finds out. He'll need someone to comfort him properly.

Chad looked around as if the neighbors might be listening to his thoughts. He shook his head but the idea was stubborn, like it wasn't the first time he'd talked himself into thinking about another woman.

She'd like him. Maybe she could convince him to cut that rat tail off.

It was settled. A young boy couldn't do without a female presence in the house. Chad stood up taller, his conscience argued into a drunken submission. He slapped his hands on the sides of his belly and listened to the hollow sound they made. That would need fixing too. He set his phone alarm to go off at six the next morning. Plenty of time for a walk. He checked the fridge and found it stocked with plenty of green things for him to eat. He threw out the beer and half the wine too.

I'm going to have to lose some weight if anyone's ever going to fuck me again.

He paused, staring into the trashcan, waiting for his conscience to raise its shamed head but there was nothing. After a moment he reached down and pulled the Budweiser out of the trash. No one could blame him for a beer or six, all things considered.

The Tava

by Radhika Borde

Rajinder was a big man. A big appetite for life. A big belly. No one sniggered at Rajinder's appetite for life. An English mistress. A Polish mistress. The young, fragile Filipino. The Czech woman who accompanied him to concerts in tight, black dresses.

And a wife who never let any of this dim the gloss of her pearls. (Rajinder gave her lots of them. Necessarily.)

If a smaller man had done it, there would have been sniggers. But Rajinder took up too much space in a room for anyone to snigger. Then there was his pride in the women. Each one a goddess. Here was a man who needed a harem. A weakness that could be indulged.

There are two sources of happiness and unhappiness in life. One is the moment. And the other is the narrative that strings the events of a life together. Rajinder so obviously enjoyed his moments that no one had the heart to pin the narrative of his adultery onto him.

He was a man who laughed a lot in public. No one had ever seen him cry.

Why then did Rajinder cry at his grand-daughter's wedding feast?

No one could console him. His wife was there. As was his Polish mistress. She had been his grand-daughter's favourite auntie – according to Amisha her grandmother's best friend. Always going on holidays together, with her grandfather tagging along with them for the things for which a man was needed. Talk that she was her grandfather's mistress was dismissed with a 'Possibly. You know *Dadaji*...'.

Second Taste

At her wedding, her grandmother and her grandmother's best friend/grandfather's mistress each clung to a big, hunched shoulder. Trying to stem the shuddering of the flesh under the expensive silk.

They weren't able to.

And the big man's tears proved to be as contagious as his laughter had always been.

To understand Rajinder's tears, we will have to go back many years – to 1947, to Lahore. When Rajinder was a little boy with lots of questions. When one country had decided that it was two.

*

When they had to leave their home in Lahore, Rajinder's family took very little with them. A few clothes, some things that could be sold, and a cast iron *tava* on which his mother said they would cook.

There really wasn't any time to pack properly. Rajinder didn't even have time to say goodbye to his pet cat. She had gone out on one of her mock hunting expeditions and he was told that they couldn't wait till she returned.

'Our neighbours will take care of her,' said his mother.

This didn't reassure him. Especially since his eavesdropping had revealed that their neighbours were the reason for their flight.

It was all very strange. Why did they have to run away from Arif and Asif, little Ameena, Uncle Rafiq, Aunty Meher and old *Dadi-jaan*? When Rajinder didn't have to go to school he would always run over to eat *sheermals* with them. They would make it for breakfast. The sweet milk-bread was something he didn't get at home. Sometimes *Dadi-jaan* would add raisins to the dough and then it would be even better. He would sit on one of the low wooden stools in their kitchen. Asif, Arif and Ameena would be sitting around him. Large brass plates balanced on their knees. *Dadi-jaan* would land a *sheermal* into each one with a light toss of her wrist. Hot off the *tava* they would come. One within seconds of the other. Crisp and flaky on the outside, soft within.

The children would wait till Rajinder's sheermal had cooled to a temperature that his fingertips could withstand. When he tore off the first piece, releasing a little cloud of fragrant steam, the other children would follow. And then they would eat. Grinning broadly at each other as they did.

'Have they become bad people now?' Rajinder had asked, when his father told him that he couldn't say goodbye to the Ibrahims. He couldn't imagine them being bad. Did *Dadi-jaan* know how to be bad? Rajinder didn't think so.

'Stop the questions Raju…no one has become bad,' his father had replied. Adding, 'the world has become bad. And you will have to grow up fast.'

This had comforted Rajinder. So, it wasn't as if they had become bad.

It was bigger than that.

Rajinder would love to talk while he ate the *sheermals* with the Ibrahims. He would pester *Dadi-jaan* with questions. And *Dadi-jaan* was happy to chatter along.

'How many sheermals can you make at one time, *Dadi-jaan*?'

'Fifteen, maybe twenty…this *tava* is big enough. But what do you need twenty for, my son? There are only four of you. By the time you have eaten your first *sheermal*, your *Dadi-jaan* will have the second ready for you.'

In time, the mornings around the Ibrahims' *tava* came to be Rajinder's most powerful memory. It protected him like a talisman. Later, he would look for glimpses of *Dadi-jaan* in his various girlfriends, his wife, and his mistresses. He would find her softness in others. Her generosity, never.

But as a five-year old in the Ibrahims' kitchen, eating the sheermals that *Dadi-jaan* had made, Rajinder lived in a simple truth – that *Dadi-jaan* made the best *sheermals* in the world and that he loved watching the glow of concentration in her face as she made them.

Of course, Rajinder would also go to the Ibrahim's house for lunches and dinners. They would all go. But then they would eat formally in the living room. It wouldn't do to sit in the kitchen on those low wooden stools. They would have to sit around a huge brass plate on a red silk carpet. The carpet would tickle the soles of Rajinder's feet, and half his enjoyment would come from watching how everyone else ate. The women always slightly shy. The men intent on their gustatory pleasure. Ameena giggling while she ate. She was never serious about her food. Not like her brothers. Their eyes would be round and moist as they plunged morsels of spiced meat into their mouths. They would eat *tak-a-tak* and soft *naan* breads. Rice cooked with nuts and dried fruit. Velvety soft meatballs simmered in rich, creamy gravies. Everything was always wonderful but the *tak-a-tak* at the Ibrahims' house was so delicious that Rajinder would eat it in his dreams. Meat and spices cooked with tomatoes, onions, and green chillies. How they would scoop up the thick gravy with those *naan* breads... Rajinder had never thought of the Ibrahims as neighbours. They were who they were and that was enough. No need for the abstract categories of family and neighbours to apply.

But now they were leaving Lahore and they were leaving the Ibrahims behind – and apparently, they had to do this as quickly as they could.

'Why are we hurrying?' Rajinder had asked his father.

'Because we have a train to catch and we have to be on time.'

'Where are we going?' was his next question.

'To Delhi,' his father replied.

Second Taste

Now this was exciting. Rajinder was curious about Delhi. His cousins had been there and their stories of it had lived and grown in his imagination.

Rajinder left the house with one hand clasped in his mother's and one eye on the curtained windows of the Ibrahims' house. He thought he saw some movement behind the lace fabric, but he was hurried away so quickly that he couldn't be sure.

A man with a horse and cart was waiting for them at the end of the road. He had picked up their luggage from their doorstep and had loaded it into the cart. They got in, squeezing themselves into whatever spaces they could find. But just as they were leaving they saw *Dadi-jaan* hurry out of her house with a large cloth bundle in her hands. She stuffed it into the cart as it was moving off and shouted after them.

'Twenty *sheermals*! Raju, I made all of them on our *tava* – all at once! May God go with you.'

And they watched as she disappeared in the dust that trailed behind them.

'What times, what times…,' said the cart driver. 'Neighbours losing trust in each other. A country divided. People's hearts are being torn apart. And what is the government doing? Spreading fear and inciting riots. They want to clear people out. And look at you. You are clearing out…'

'Before anything can happen,' said his father curtly. 'We are not going to wait for that. We have heard the reports. And anyway, there can't be a place for us in this new country. This Pakistan. Lahore will always be our Lahore. But our leaders have decided our fate for us. We have no choice.'

'Yes, our great leaders…,' said the cart driver. 'Make no mistake, they will take the place of the British masters. All this talk of independence. But what does it mean for your family? The only thing it means is that you have to flee. Is this the great independence that we have been striving for?'

And the two men talked bitterly of the times as they trundled towards the station. All the while Rajinder cradled the bundle of *sheermals* that *Dadi-jaan* had given them. He could smell the hot, yeasty dough through the cloth, and it warmed his arms and lap.

When they got to the station they saw that it was a knotted mass of people and luggage. There wasn't even place to stand. It really did look as if no more people could be added to the platforms.

They pushed their way to the train.

'We are going to ride in the luggage van,' his father shouted out behind him as he elbowed a path through the writhing mass.

'Why the luggage van, Mummy?' Rajinder asked his mother.

'No questions... no questions,' she answered, through a clenched mouth.

When they got to the luggage van, the ticket collector was waiting for them. Rajinder recognized him. He had seen him in their house on a couple of occasions. The ticket collector would drink tea in his father's office. Now, he saw him whispering into his father's ear through his heavy moustache. His father nodded. All of them clambered onto the luggage van and hauled their luggage into it one by one. Then his father proceeded to arrange their luggage in the shape of an L, in the farthest corner of the van.

'Sit down inside it,' he said to Rajinder.

'Why, it's just like a fortress,' said Rajinder.

'Exactly,' said his father.

Other people got onto the luggage van. All of them were known to the conductor. They tried to do something similar with their luggage, but when Rajinder stood up and peered at their efforts, he decided that their fortress was the best. After all, they had a *tava* right at the front. Like a big shield. Just as big as the *tava Dadi-jaan* would cook her *sheermals* on.

Second Taste

When the train was groaning with people, it slipped away from the platform. There was a lot of shouting as it left. Rajinder couldn't understand the words, but something about the noise made him uneasy.

'Have a *sheermal*,' his mother advised as she stroked his forehead with a damp palm.

And he did.

The sweet, flaky dough and the *thaka thak thak-thaka thak thak* of the train's wheels as they passed over the fish plates made Rajinder sleepy.

He slept.

Through several of the stops on the way, at which more people tried to get onto the train.

Through the shouts of the gangs that were patrolling the train tracks and attacking the trains they were able to jump onto.

But he didn't sleep through the bullets that managed to penetrate the slats in the side of the luggage van.

The explosions of the gunpowder woke him.

As did his father's loud voice and strong arms as they pulled him behind their *tava*.

'Ping! Ping! Ping!' went the bullets.

Making music with their violent intent against the heavy iron of the cooking utensil.

Rajinder would grow up to remember this as an exhilarating experience. When it was happening, he knew that they would win against the attackers. They had their *tava*. *Tavas* had given Rajinder too much life for him to doubt their strength. And he was right. It didn't let them down.

Second Taste

When they arrived in Delhi, the *tava* was the one constant in the complex equation determining their survival. They were refugees who would live in the courtyards of their relatives' houses. But the *tava* was big enough for them, and for others. Rajinder would watch the hot air shimmer above it every evening and would think that a day would come when rich meats would be cooked on it just as they had been in Lahore.

In this, he was correct. But abundance is more than material, and there remained a feeling of loss that Rajinder could never shake off.

The loss followed Rajinder to England. No *sheermals* in England. But a job as a foreman in a small textile factory was available for his father. All of it organized by a distant relative who lived there. Clan loyalties like ballast in their turbulent lives.

Rajinder's father began work at the factory. And Rajinder began school. It was hard for them both at the start, but they shared a habit of showing up and saying yes. And this got them through.

Children of Polish immigrants, English children who had experienced the war as babies, children like Rajinder – all in a class together. Bombed out buildings and rationed food.

But then there came the gains. For both Rajinder and his father. For them all.

A fabric shop opened. A scholarship. More businesses. Rajinder's mother was speaking English now – a working woman. A place at university for Rajinder. Did it obliterate the loss? No. But it buried it deep.

In the Punjabi business community in Birmingham, weddings are more a proclamation of status and wealth than of anything else. An unlikely situation in which to expose vulnerability. But perhaps Rajinder had arrived so comfortably that he really didn't care.

And so Rajinder cried at his grand-daughter's wedding. Everyone thought he was crying for the loss of his grand-daughter to her husband's family. This would have been somewhat

Second Taste

appropriate. They cried with him for this. His wife dabbing at her eyes with the brocade hem of her *sari*. His mistress furiously blinking back tears – she didn't want them running through her mascara.

But this wasn't why he was crying. Rajinder wouldn't cry for the loss of his granddaughter. 'Unable to enjoy life,' he had told his wife after several meals at which he had seen her picking at her food. 'It's different when a girl is naturally thin.'

No one knew. Rajinder never told them. He wouldn't have been able to articulate the truth. That he was crying for everything that he had experienced around a *tava*.

There it was at his grand-daughter's wedding feast.

Spiced mutton was cooking on it, and everyone was eating with relish.

Second Taste

Radhika Borde is currently teaching and writing in Central Europe. She has a PhD in Cultural Geography from Wageningen University in the Netherlands. Her flash story *Triple Goddess* was published by Tin House (online). She researches issues related to the intersections between nature and culture and works with an international group of the International Union for Conservation of Nature which specializes in this. Radhika believes that food is an important junction at which nature and culture intersect – with potential for bringing people together.

Website: https://radhikaborde.wixsite.com/website

Solving Torrent's Equation

by Jeremy Forge

To become autonomous is to take control of your learning.

That's what Magnus told me. Even the Japanese can be autonomous, he said. Magnus is a great believer in autonomy. *Autonomous Learning* by Magnus Torrent. Not on the bestseller lists, to be sure, but it's earned him the right to get invited to international conferences.

But I'm not in Japan now, I'm somewhere above Siberia. A man with a wooden leg has just shot another man and Matt Damon is furious. 'What the fuck did you do that for?' he screams. I have to press the earplugs tight to catch the reply: 'You can't come here and make our decisions for us.' Matt's jaw drops as if at last he understands what the film's all about.

I could cite enough revolting facts about chickens to fill a book twice the size of Torrent's. They get one hour of darkness a day and half a square foot to live in. They get fat so quickly their legs buckle and break. By the time they die, two thirds are infected with campylobacter. They have skin infections and ammonia burns and foamy exudate in their eyes. I could go on. In fact I used to go on and on: botulism, cannibalism, breast blister, swollen head disease – you name it.

And now, do I give a fuck? No. I've given up my vegan phase. An hour out of Tokyo they gave us tikka masala and it went down a treat.

Daddy died unexpectedly. At forty-eight, he decided to give us his final lesson: this is what comes of not looking after yourself. OK, he stopped smoking a while ago, but he coated every mouthful with salt and washed it down with Burgundy. That was after the whisky he drank before.

People liked Daddy. A man of heart. The way they speak of him, you'd think he had the biggest heart in the world. Perhaps he did. Or perhaps he was simply asking it to do too much.

And yet – get this – he had a head for business too. A rare combination, said Des. You don't get many like that.

Des Meakin. The linchpin of Lecky & Son. The welfare and cleanliness of broilers has been his major concern for forty years. When I was young, I thought a flock-keeper dipped his hand into bags of grain and tossed it to the chickens, like my Gran with the hens in her yard. But it's all about damage containment. That means litter. You can't keep it clean because it only gets changed when the flock's taken off to be killed, but still you can minimise infection, and that's what Des is good at. And taking away the ones that die nonetheless.

I've got five days to decide. Chickens or Japanese students? My first appearance in front of the class was a flop. 'Work in pairs,' I said. 'Interview each other. Your interests, your goals, your ambitions. Who are you? Who do you want to be? That's what I want to know.'

Silence. They stared at me as if I'd stepped out of a spaceship.

Magnus has been helpful. He's been in Japan eight years and knows a trick or two. He tells me becoming autonomous is like solving a magic equation: get the terms right and the solution is greater than the sum of its parts. This is surely profound and I'm grateful to him for the insight, but I wish he wouldn't talk at me as if I'm the audience at a plenary session in Sydney or Singapore. He doesn't do that when he speaks with Teri. He asks her questions and listens to her and laughs. Teri and Magnus are both from Vancouver. I sense there's a bond between them, even though the Torrent family (as Magnus has said many times) are old Vancouverites, while Teri's mother arrived in the 70s from Saigon. So now whenever he sees us together, I'm holding Teri's hand. Just to make sure he knows.

'I may not come back.' I said this to Teri because I wanted to be honest. We've been going out for three months. Our relationship thrives on Tokyo's buzz and the strangeness of things. It isn't yet ready for death or decisions. Forty-eight was too early for everyone.

'I'm the heir now, you see.' She nodded, but I don't think she did. 'I mean, technically speaking, my mother is, but I'll be the one to step in.' I left a pause which lasted three seconds, but contained my whole future. 'If I want to.'

I don't know what I was expecting. 'Come back to me, Simon, please. You won't regret it, I promise. And if you prefer to stay in England, I'll follow you. There's so much you and I have to live for.' Some sort of fantasy like that. But what she did was look at me for a while without saying anything. Then she nodded and said, 'I guess you'll decide what's best.'

And now we're lined up outside the church and the ceremony is over, the inside bit anyway. It carries on here outside, the shaking hands and condolences, huddled under umbrellas. I'm in the middle, Mummy on my right, Lucy, my kid sister, on my left. Except she's not a kid any more, she's eighteen, and blessed with a shape she gets a kick from seeing people notice.

I'm over it now, but half way through Corinthians, my strong and confident voice broke down. For several seconds, with all eyes upon me, I gazed at the ceiling, desperate to shake my fist and howl, 'What the fuck did you do that for?'

I got the strong and confident voice from Marlborough. 'Here ends the lesson,' went echoing round the chapel till the organ chords kicked in. They were good at giving us strong and confident voices. The rest was another matter.

My parents were very proud of me going to Marlborough, which I think in their minds had something to do with calling them Mummy and Daddy. It worried them stiff when I went through a phase of insisting on Mum and Dad.

Second Taste

Eight or so down the line is Jimmy Sharp and behind him, Des Meakin. I knew about that, because Daddy told me he'd hired Jimmy Sharp and Des was showing him the ropes. But it never sank in till now, as I watch them shuffle towards me, softly chatting. There's something about it I find indecent, something which sets me on edge, and yet it contains a logic which can't be denied: Jimmy can be mates with Des in a way that I never could. The closer they get, the harder it is to concentrate on the handshakes.

Mummy releases Meredith the butcher and passes him onto me. I nod, smile sadly, say 'Thank you.' Sympathy taken like the sweets passed round as the plane prepares to land. But my eyes all the while are darting in the direction of Jimmy and Des.

Jimmy Sharp. There was Doug, Tommy, Brian and Gus, but most of all there was Jimmy. My parents didn't approve of him – a ruffian. Well, that's what Mummy said – Daddy was never there to approve or disapprove. In the playground once, Jimmy came up and demanded my Pokémon and got me in an arm lock when I refused. But I twisted free and hooked a foot round his ankle and tipped him flat on his back. My life was in danger after that, so I stopped going out during break, till the headmaster noticed it and asked to speak to Mummy.

'Oh, he's a ruffian, that one,' she said. 'Takes after his father. But I don't see the problem. You've beaten him once, Simon Lecky – are you trying to tell me you can't do it again? What are you so worried about?'

Simply this: I didn't know how I'd done it, I knew I couldn't do it again, and Jimmy had a whole gang behind him.

So naturally, I was wary when Doug Willis came up in the break and said, 'We're going out after school. Want to come?'

'Out?'

'Exploring. Me and Jimmy and the others.'

'I don't know. I usually go straight home.'

Second Taste

'Jimmy says you're good. He told me what happened.' Doug was Jimmy's deputy and he didn't just have a catapult, he had a Swiss knife with a file, a corkscrew and six different ways of cutting.

'Well, yeah... A bit of luck maybe, but... OK, why not?' Never did a shrug so non-committal conceal such a jubilant heart. Throw Jimmy Sharp to the ground and what do you get? Respect. You get drafted into the gang.

At the beginning, the son in Lecky & Son was my father. I was still a baby when he moved up from Son to Lecky, but the name was kept like a permanent invitation. And now it's decision time.

A couple of years ago, it would have been a no-brainer. I said to Daddy, 'How can you? It's fucking immoral!' It made him wince, but he didn't argue. There wasn't any point. I was drunk.

Now I've grown up, I don't have the rage any more. Of course it's revolting, but they're a source of protein and Lecky & Son provides a livelihood for twenty-six employees.

When I joined the animal rights brigade, it wasn't that I was bothered about the chickens. I wanted to know who I was. Maybe I was running away from myself, hoping to mutate. We'd sit around and talk about letter bombs and I felt loony and uplifted at once. 'Yeah, let's nuke 'em,' I said, and this girl I fancied gave me a withering look and told me to grow up.

So I did.

Jimmy's handshake is firm and his other hand squeezes my forearm. 'Simon,' is all he says – three parts greeting, and the rest up to me to interpret. There has to be condolence, but is it just me, or is there a hint of a challenge? And those little brackets at the corner of his lips – are they what's keeping the smile within bounds he assumes are decent? It's over so quickly and even before he lets go, his eyes have moved on to Lucy.

Then it's Des Meakin. He stares at me so dolefully that for a moment my bereavement is sucked into his: it isn't me who's lost his father but Des, and he's standing there helpless as a puppy, unable to speak, till eventually I say, 'Des... I was so sorry to hear about Mrs. Meakin.'

She used to work for my parents too. She cleaned our house and when Mummy went out she looked after me and Lucy. When I was six and odious and trying to figure things out, I asked her why, and when she told me, I said, 'Oh, so really you're my servant.' I can still see the shock that crumpled her face. Then it recovered its smile, as if what I'd said was really quite sweet, and would later be told as a joke.

You never thought of Des and Mrs Meakin as being married. Des was Des and she was Mrs. Meakin. Perhaps her name was Mary – I'm not sure. Sometimes I'd see them together in their sitting room, but Des was so much younger that he might have been a nephew who'd come to visit. It would have been different if they'd had children of their own, but that was hard to imagine. Des had sandy hair and a shiny face, and whenever I saw him he was smiling. Mrs. Meakin smiled too, but her hair was white and her face was fleshy and florid. I knew they were husband and wife, but they weren't like other couples, the friends of my parents who paid no attention to me. Des and Mrs Meakin always looked as if they were waiting for someone to give them permission to hug me.

Did I mention his wife to stop him poaching on my grief? Or rather – more likely – to remind him how thoughtless I am. Almost a year since she died, and no one else's letter, I know, would have meant as much as mine. But I never wrote.

It works: he registers pain. *Now, after all this time? A single, pathetic, inadequate sentence, spoken between two handshakes? And if your father hadn't died, there wouldn't even be that.*

Second Taste

But no, that's not what he's thinking, or at least it doesn't get that far. Des has an inbuilt sprinkler, the same as his wife's, ready to douse any spark of misgiving related to a Lecky. In less than a second the puppy is back, telling me I'm the anointed heir to his allegiance and devotion.

The bridge on Station Road – I'd crossed it a thousand times but never walked beneath; nor been inside the signal box on the disused railway track. Everything looks different when you're a member of the gang.

That was the first time. The second time Jimmy said, 'Where's your air rifle?'

I'd mentioned it to Doug. My birthday present. I said I could hit a Zubes tin from fifty yards. The tin was true but not the fifty yards. Maybe fifteen.

'It's broken.'

'Liar,' said Jimmy. I thought he was going to make me go home and get it, but he turned to the rest of the gang. 'OK, let's go.'

We didn't go exploring, we went to the Meakins'. I was already worried – I should have been home for my trumpet lesson – but when we got to the Meakins', the worry turned into wanting to be sick.

They took out their catapults. First to smash a tulip was the winner. It wasn't easy because the tulips were a dozen yards off and to get a good angle, they had to stand on the bottom rung of the fence, so they only had a few seconds before losing balance. Stone after stone went whizzing past and thudded into the patch of lawn beyond. The others hooted with every miss, but they didn't know that before each aim, my whole body was tensed in prayer, willing the stone to go wide.

Second Taste

I stood on my own, knowing I wasn't part of the gang, that in fact I never had been, yet unable to fully accept it, as if this was just a misunderstanding, and any minute now they'd realise the error of their ways. But Jimmy Sharp had understood only too well.

'Here.' When he thrust the catapult at me, it wasn't an offer but an order.

'No, it's all right, I...'

'What's the matter? I'm letting you have a go.'

'Thanks, but it's OK, honestly.'

'Something wrong? You should have brought your air rifle, shouldn't you? Still, maybe you're just as good with a catapult. Come on, show us how it's done.'

I aimed to miss, but not the way that I did. When the stone flopped a couple of yards away, the jeers made me cry with fury and hatred and shame. I filled my pocket with ammunition and shot it off in rapid succession, missing each time, but outdoing all the others in rage and despair.

There came a sound of shattering glass. Jimmy said, 'Hey! You've smashed the greenhouse!'

It wasn't possible – the greenhouse was yards away. So I knew it was them, and I was right: they were lobbing stones at it, and the glass was showering down inside, and I ran at them, screaming to stop it.

The front door opened. They fled. And that was how the Meakins saw me, gaping at the ruined greenhouse, before I flung the catapult to the ground and ran away too.

There must be over a hundred people, seated at trestle tables, each with a bouquet of flowers and a photograph of Daddy. I suppose this is part of the ceremony too, communal devouring of Lecky's

Second Taste

Chicken Kiev as a sign that life goes on. People approach me and say yet again how sorry they are, what a wonderful man he was. I'm not even sure who some of them are, but they seem to have known him well. All of the staff are there too, some of them close to retirement. A few, like Des, started when my Granddad was running the business.

The room is full of swirling, relentless chatter, and for a moment I get the horrible vision that we're cooped up here to cluck away endlessly till we die. Above the whole gathering hangs the invisible equation: find the unknown term in Lecky and Son.

It's 11 p.m. in Tokyo, and all of a sudden I want to be with Teri. Or rather I want her here, I want her to meet Des Meakin and measure the expectation in his smile. Because all I've done with her is surf on the present of Tokyo, marvelling at the fabric of its extravagance: Shibuya clubbers, shoppers in Ginza, and those pale as porcelain slips of Japanese girls with their plastic macs and accessorised nails and bouffed up orange hair, falling asleep over mobile phones in the subway. But now I want to show her my past and I want to see hers. I want to know what she did in Vancouver that made her the way she is, and what she knows of her mother's life in Saigon. I want to swap tales of childhood. Perhaps if I tell her everything, she'll understand me better than I do myself.

So I slink away and find a computer and that's more or less what I write. There's a chance she'll still be up, so I dash it off and trust in spontaneity. It's not a proposal, and nor do I say I love her. It's a plea and an offer and a hope, and it goes much deeper than anything I've ever said to her out loud.

Or maybe I'm simply missing her lips, and her body pressed close to mine.

'It seemed the obvious thing.' I'm back in search of that unknown term, and Mummy's attempting an answer, smoking with little, dainty puffs, holding the cigarette close to her lips and not inhaling.

It makes her look neurotic, or perhaps she's giving herself airs. She's always been like that. She writes poems and speaks in a drawl and manages to look condescending even when she smiles. 'Until you had your moment of madness with that...' She tosses her head and waves away the very concept: she knows the word 'animal' and she knows the word 'rights', but she can't put the two together. 'Which of course your father was very disappointed about. But times change, don't they? And young people think they know all the answers. Or at least they want to go looking for themselves. Thus has it ever been.'

This is a typical answer from Mummy, who, except when it comes to broilers, is a great believer in freedom. Until I spoke about these things with Magnus, I used to assume that freedom and autonomy were the same. But freedom is what you're given or denied by others, the ones in power. You can't be autonomous unless you're free, but freedom isn't enough. At times you'll also need a guiding hand, a message of warmth and support, and that isn't something that Mummy has ever been good at.

Or to put it another way: 'Warmth?' shrieks Lucy. 'We grew up in a fucking igloo!'

She says it too loud and she's drunk too much, so I take her outside and we sit on a bench and she tells me I'd be mad. 'Stuck in this dump for the rest of your life? With chickens? Oh, Simon, come on!'

'No, I think... It could be moved on, you know? Free range. It isn't just the ethical stuff. There's a market now. It's a matter of common sense.'

But Lucy takes no interest in broilers. She wants to talk about Freshers' Week and the student bar and boyfriends coming to blows. I don't know how much she's studying, but as far as the rest of it goes, she's taken perfect control of her learning.

Second Taste

I feel quite staid in comparison, but I talk all the same about Teri, and the time we got up at five to visit the fish market, and afterwards, over miso soup, I described the inside of a chicken shed.

Lucy listens and then says to me that the way I speak of her, it sounds as if I'm in love.

'I love it when she laughs, you know? She's just so beautiful when she laughs.'

Actually, no, that's wrong. What I mean is her laugh is a puff of gold, sparkling in a beauty she has all the time.

And now it's all over and we go back home and retreat to separate rooms. Perhaps that's the way it should be, each of us coming to terms with it on our own. I wonder what Mummy's doing. Writing a poem? *Ode to a loved one who died too young.* On second thoughts, no. More likely a letter to her lover.

She told me just now she's already had a call from Tinkham's. To express their sympathy, of course, but also to remind her that as a leading UK poultry company, they're in a position to make her a very good offer. 'Just imagine, though,' she added as she went up the stairs, 'if we sold out to Tinkham's, how utterly devastated poor Des Meakin would be.'

Teri is fast asleep now. I take a deep breath, picturing her head on the pillow, her mouth just slightly open. I log in to my mailbox.

Thank you for your lovely message, Simon, it brought tears to my eyes as I read it. I think of you having to deal with your father's death, how very difficult it must be, and I would indeed have liked to be by your side to help you through the ordeal. But of course it wasn't a practical proposition, and we really haven't known each other for that long. Yes, there's a lot we still could share, and I do hope we get the chance. But now the decision you have to take is so big, and my part in your life has been so small, that it wouldn't be right to have me in mind when you take it. You mustn't stake your future on me, Simon. I would feel terrible if you came back to Japan and it didn't work out between us, and really, to be honest, I think to do that would be putting too much pressure on me. I've so enjoyed discovering Tokyo with you, but perhaps that's because there have been no expectations. But now it suddenly feels as if there's a huge commitment to make, and I really don't know if I can make it.

I remember you telling me about your first class, and asking your students who they were and who they wanted to be. And I think that now these are questions you must be asking yourself. What I'm saying is I'm sure you'll find the right answer, but whatever equation it is you have to solve, it wouldn't be right to include me as one of its terms.

Thinking of you and missing you,

Teri.

It's getting dark as I drive down to the compound. Teri's message turns in my mind, but the flimsy fragments I cling to for hope are pulled down by all the rest. And nothing heavier than the weighted sack of Magnus Torrent's equation.

I wanted to be on my own. To see what it feels like to stand outside the long, low sheds and think of myself as the Lecky in Lecky & Son, keeping the second slot warm for an unborn heir. But another car is parked there, and I'm wondering who it belongs to when Des and Jimmy appear round the corner of the shed. What are they here for? Reassurance? Solace? To check that the chickens haven't all died of grief? They were deep in conversation, but on seeing me they stop. We face each other through a tense, uncertain twilight, and it feels so like a film that my brain automatically generates the screenplay:

Second Taste

'I'm taking over. We're going free range.' Pause. 'You hear what I say, Jimmy Sharp?'

'Yeah, I hear.' Looking up slowly, eyes narrowed. 'But listen to me now, Lecky. You can't come here and make our decisions for us.'

A pair of crows, wings thrashing, bolt from a nearby tree. The two men go for their guns.

But what happens in the real world is that Jimmy bows his head, listening to Des murmur briefly in his ear. Then he straightens up and walks towards me, cigarette tucked in the corner of his mouth. He stops a few feet away. 'Funny how things turn out.' I don't know what he means by that, but I nod. He reaches out and taps me on the shoulder. 'You'll do fine. You'll do as good as your Dad.' And before I can answer he walks on to his car.

As Jimmy turns the key, Des goes to join him, and for a moment his face is caught in the glare of the headlights. The way his hair has receded gives it an oblong shape. It makes me think of a slate that needs to be written on, needs to be fierce with fury and hatred and spite. But he turns towards me and there's that smile, telling me all is forgiven, that nothing ever happened to the greenhouse, there never was anything to forgive.

I've become the person he's always wanted me to be.

*

I sent my letter ten days ago from Bangkok. Des should have got it by now. It was long and carefully worded, but I don't know if I really managed to explain. I told him about Mae Sot, where I'm heading, and the camps full of refugees. I wasn't sure how much he knows about Burma, so I told him about the conditions there, and how the Karen people who escape into Thailand are free at last, but in need of warmth and support. I said I'd be giving them classes in English, and I didn't know how long I'd stay, but I said it felt right, as if I've found the person I am and the person I want to be. I said that I'd finally taken control of my learning.

Second Taste

What I didn't say was how the smiling slate of his face, that evening after the funeral, told me the very opposite of what he intended. It told me that to become myself, I had to break out of the shed in which I was trapped.

As for Teri, it's taking a while, but I'm getting over her now. And maybe I'm totally wrong, but to help me do that, I tell myself she's surely making excellent progress in algebra.

Second Taste

Jeremy Forge currently lives in Hokkaido, Japan, where he raises chickens autonomously and works from time to time on *The Novel That Will Never Be Finished.* He writes short stories which he submits to competitions, but omits to read the rules about maximum word count.

Second Taste

The Gold Mystery

by Brian Gosling

We don't have a very good time of it, I'm afraid. At first I didn't even realise – I thought nothing existed outside of the cage. Well, the other cages, obviously, and twice a day Gold coming in to feed us, but He's so different from us, I never even tried to imagine what His life was like. When you live in such a restricted environment, it really affects your brain, I can tell you. A couple of square feet is all I've got, I can't even turn round. The same view all the time, the inside of the Barn. It's nice enough, I'm not saying that, but after a few weeks, you know every tiny detail. No stimulation at all. I'd love to turn round, see what's behind me, but Gold will never let us do that. It would take too long to feed us if He did.

A few weeks ago, this rumour went around. Or rather it got passed along the row, because that's how it is here, one straight line stretching Mother Goose knows how far. I guess I'm somewhere in the middle, so what with all the honking, what got passed along to me could be totally different from the start. Anyway, apparently there's an Outside. There's something out there beyond the Barn. I don't know if it's true, but the rumour was that one of us pretended to be dead, and as soon as he got outside, he waddled off. Gold caught him pretty quickly and brought him back, but there's things out there... I can hardly begin to imagine. It's green, they say, green all over, except for the roof which is really high up, and blue. You can turn around, you can look in all directions, and it never ends. And up in the roof there's a light so bright it hurts your eyes to look at it. There's so much space, you can put one foot in front of the other, you can waddle! Imagine that! No one's ever done it here but everyone's got the urge. It wouldn't matter where, just move, you know, go somewhere. Wow!

Maybe it was all invented. I don't know. But we all believe in it. We want it to be true, if not for us, then for future generations. There's nothing wrong with dreaming, is there? And logically, it

Second Taste

makes sense, because when Gold's finished feeding us and He disappears through a door, He must go somewhere, mustn't He? No one had ever come up with a decent answer as to where – the most popular theory was that He only became visible in the Barn, and the door led to a sort of non-Gold, or essence of Gold, that surrounded the Barn. Like everyone else, I'd always thought there was only the Barn, and Gold created the Barn and all that was in it. But if there's an Outside, it forces us into a radical rethink. Did Gold create the Outside too? In which case, what position does the Barn hold in His system? Perhaps we're not at the centre, as was thought, but there are other Barns out there too. Ever since we heard about it, there's been a lot of speculation about the Outside. A lot of geese think Gold will take them there one day, but personally I'm dubious. I think we're stuck in the Barn, so basically we have to make the most of it. If Gold was going to take us Outside, why did He capture the goose that escaped? He never actually tells us anything, he doesn't honk at all, in fact. That's where the name comes from, by the way – we have this saying, 'Honking is silver, silence is gold.' He's a complete mystery to us.

We're fed twice a day. Since there's nothing else that ever happens, you'd expect feeding time to be the high point of our day, but I have very ambivalent feelings towards it, to be honest. On the one hand, I'm pretty famished by the time Gold comes around, so it's great to be full again – makes me feel all drowsy and contented. Sometimes I even manage to have a little nap afterwards, though with the ones waiting to be fed honking away like crazy, I rarely get to snatch more than a few minutes. On the other hand, it's extremely unpleasant – I really hope one day Gold invents another way of feeding us. Basically what happens is He puts a hand through the bars of the cage, grabs you by the neck and pulls it till it's stretched out straight. Then as soon as you open your beak, he plunges this pipe inside and pushes it right down to your tummy. It's really nasty. Makes you want to throw up, but of course you can't because of the pipe. And then you think you're going to suffocate and your throat gets really sore. Thankfully, it only lasts a few seconds. He presses a button and in spews this great dollop of Mother Goose knows what, some sort of mash or puree, I imagine, we don't actually get to taste it so I can't say. Then there's a heavy sensation in your tummy and you feel kind of bloated, but that doesn't last too long and afterwards, like I said, you're satisfied and replete. And then once that feeling goes, you start looking forward to the next dollop.

You hear these stories about what it was like in olden times, before Gold invented the button. He took you between His knees and pulled your head up and shoved this funnel in and then turned a handle to get all the stuff to go down. Took absolutely ages apparently, so at least I can say I'm glad to have been born when I was.

Another rumour I've heard is that on the Outside, there aren't just geese but other creatures too, some that have four legs, some that fly, some that are really tiny but have six legs – weird things like that. And they don't get fed with a pipe, they feed themselves by picking things off the ground, you know, just bits of stuff lying there for them to eat when they feel like it. I don't know. I find that hard to believe, but anything's possible, I suppose.

So that's my day, basically – my life. I mean, nothing changes from one day to the next, so I've come to accept that this is all there is. Obviously you wonder what it's all for, why Gold created the Barn and filled it with geese, but no one's come up with a satisfactory answer that I know of. What does Gold do when He's fed us? And who feeds Gold? He's pretty big, so you'd need a much longer pipe than ours to get to his tummy. But maybe there are pipes like that somewhere, I don't know. Perhaps he feeds himself with the bits of things lying around Outside. If He doesn't, then there has to be some other creature feeding Him with a pipe, and the question then is who feeds the other creature? It's an infinite regress, and that sort of thing makes my head spin, so I try not to think about it too much.

Second Taste

Gold contemplates the Great Outside

Second Taste

What happened to the cats?

Powerful, mysterious, comical, adorable – the cats in these 21 stories prowl and purr their way to a truly exquisite anthology.

Each story is accompanied by original illustrations and the collection is prefaced by Smith, the terrifying tabby from Taunton who, when he's not fighting other cats, likes nothing more than to read.

Cat Tales is available in print and as an ebook. It can also be obtained directly from my website: curtisbaussebooks.com. The proceeds from this book go to the Against Malaria Foundation.

Second Taste

Fancy a trip to Pluto? Or a fearful drive along a stretch of country road? Unless you prefer to go to church with a strange woman in green tights, her hair alive with electricity. Here you have 34 stories, each one a journey, whether funny or frightening, real or figurative, shared or dreadfully alone. 'They had a long journey ahead of them' was the prompt: the writers here, from award-winning authors to exciting new talents, took it and made it their own. Sit back and enjoy the scenery, then, as the stories here open your eyes to destinations you'll want to go back to again. Bon voyage!

The proceeds from *With Our Eyes Open* go to the Against Malaria Foundation.

The book is available in print and as an ebook or direct from my website: curtisbaussebooks.com

Printed in Poland
by Amazon Fulfillment
Poland Sp. z o.o., Wrocław